PUFFIN BOOKS
Editor: Kaye Webb

PROFESSOR BRANESTAWM'S GREAT REVOLUTION

and Other Incredible Adventures

'Well, that's one invention of mine that hasn't given any trouble,' said Professor Branestawm with satisfaction, not to mention relief. The occasion was the formal opening of his Automatic Christmas Decorations, and they really hadn't shown any catastrophic drawbacks (yet!).

Yes, the Professor certainly was accident-prone, though terribly well-intentioned. There was his marvellous lost-property-finding machine, for instance, that kept finding things before they were even lost, his splendid new tank that could withstand attacks of every kind except one – from marmalade – and the unfortunate episode when he wanted to summon the plumber's aid with his pipes but received numbers of enthusiastic tartan-clad bagpipers instead. And as for his omelette-making machine, that was the worst of the lot when it took over the kitchen!

Poor Professor, and poor everyone else who was enmeshed or tangled or trapped, puzzled or perturbed, downright frustrated, chivvied, chased or even shipwrecked by his revolutionary inventions. And thank heavens for his loyal band of friends, the gallant Colonel Dedshott, Commander Hardaport and Mrs Flittersnoop, his unfailing tactful housekeeper, who are as devoted to him after all these years as the band of readers who have followed his disastrous exploits.

D1380315

NORMAN HUNTER

Professor Branestawm's
Great Revolution

AND OTHER
INCREDIBLE ADVENTURES

*

Illustrated by George Adamson

PUFFIN BOOKS

in association with The Bodley Head

Puffin Books, Penguin Books Ltd, Harmondsworth, Middlesex, England
Penguin Books, 625 Madison Avenue, New York, New York 10022, U.S.A.
Penguin Books Australia Ltd, Ringwood, Victoria, Australia
Penguin Books Canada Ltd, 2801 John Street, Markham, Ontario, Canada L3R 1B4
Penguin Books (N.Z.) Ltd, 182–190 Wairau Road, Auckland 10, New Zealand

—

First published by The Bodley Head 1974

—

Published in Puffin Books 1977

—

Copyright © Norman Hunter, 1974
Illustrations copyright © George Adamson, 1977
All rights reserved

—

Made and printed in Great Britain by
Hazell Watson & Viney Ltd, Aylesbury, Bucks
Set in Monotype Baskerville

TO THE

CHILDREN'S LIBRARIANS

IN BRITAIN AND

OVERSEAS

Contents

Acknowledgement

The idea for the machine in 'Where Are My Glasses?' came from Stephen Jourdan of Stanmore.

'Mrs Flittersnoop's Birthday Present' was first published in *Puffin Post* in 1972, and 'Professor Branestawm Goes Cuckoo' was first published in the *Puffin Annual 1974*.

I

Where Are My Glasses?

'MRS FLITTERSNOOP!' called the Professor to his housekeeper. 'Have you seen my glasses?'

Now if Mrs Flittersnoop had been the Professor she would probably have said, 'Yes', because, of course, she had seen the Professor's glasses many times. But, not being the Professor, she knew that what he meant was, 'Do you know where my glasses are?' and so she said, 'No.'

Then she said, 'Which pair?' But that didn't really help because she didn't know where any of the Professor's five pairs of glasses were.

'Where can they be?' the Professor muttered, pushing papers about on his desk and looking behind clocks and in vases, and in all the places where his glasses might be but weren't, as well as in a great many places where they couldn't possibly have been, and weren't.

'This is most annoying!' he said. 'Just as I was going to read the er, um, now what was it I was going to read?' But he found he couldn't remember that either. So instead he opened a parcel he thought had just come by post. In fact it was really a parcel he had packed up himself to send to the Society for Studying Plums of Unusual Shape, with two plums of unusual shape Mrs

Flittersnoop had bought with some others for making a pie.

He found that the parcel contained his five pairs of glasses, which he had wrapped up carefully by mistake while eating the plums. He put all the glasses on just as Mrs Flittersnoop came downstairs with an armful of washing.

'Well, there now,' she said. 'You've got your glasses on all the time.'

'Oh, er, have I?' he said, putting his hand up and knocking all the pairs of glasses off.

'You know, sir,' she said. 'If I might make so bold, I think you should invent one of your inventions for finding your glasses when you've lost them. It would save a great deal of time, I'm sure, sir.' She put four of the Professor's pairs of glasses into his different pockets and one pair on his nose.

'Why, er, yes, I suppose it would,' murmured the Professor. 'I, er, that is to say . . . my goodness, Mrs Flittersnoop, that's a wonderful idea! I think you should patent it.'

And he went away to think about something entirely different. Mrs Flittersnoop followed him into his study and said, 'A machine for finding lost glasses, sir. That's what you ought to invent, if you don't mind my saying so.'

'Ha!' said the Professor suddenly. 'An idea has just struck me. I shall invent a machine for finding my glasses when I lose them. Don't you think that's a wonderful idea, Mrs, er, Flittersnoop?'

But Mrs Flittersnoop had gone away to attend to the laundry and was already beginning to wish she had a machine for finding where the Professor had put his yesterday's shirt.

Inventing the great spectacle-finding machine proved a little difficult because the Professor kept thinking of other sensational ideas and the machine became in turn a thing for picking pears off the top of high trees where the best ones always grow, a device for making television programmes look better than they were, which he found it impossible to complete, and then a machine for taking to supermarkets to work out how much things cost after allowing for so many pence off and offers of three for the price of two and a free gift. But as this machine was six feet square and weighed two tons, the Professor felt it wasn't quite as practical as it might have been, and managed to get back on the glasses invention.

At last he had it finished. It had a two-way telescope with electronic focusing device, part of a submarine detector that his next-door neighbour, Commander Hardaport (Retired), had loaned to him, a smell-sensitive electric eye which would find anything as long as you knew what it smelt like and set the dial accordingly, and a thermostat for preventing it from getting too hot when it was hot on the trail of spectacles.

'Well, I must say it looks very nice, sir,' said Mrs Flittersnoop, when the Professor brought his spectacle-finding machine in to show her. 'It reminds me rather of a dog my sister Aggie once had. It was sort of part Alsatian, part Yorkshire terrier with some bits of bull-dog and Pekingese, although some said it was more like a wire-haired Pomeranian.'

'Er, dogs did you say, Mrs Flittersnoop?' muttered the Professor, fiddling with the machine. 'Well, ah, of course, this could possibly be classed as some kind of retriever.'

'Yes, indeed, I'm sure sir,' said Mrs Flittersnoop, not being quite certain whether the Professor meant it to be a joke or not.

'It has to have legs,' explained the Professor, patting the machine, which wagged its radio aerial to show it was pleased, 'because it may have to go up and down stairs looking for my glasses and, of course, wheels would not have done.'

'It looks a bit like one of those great big dogs that have barrels of brandy hung round their necks for rescuing people lost in the mountains,' said Mrs Flitter-snoop.

'St Bernards,' said the Professor. 'Yes, that is where I got the idea. The basket is for the machine to carry the spectacles so that they do not get damaged. It simply picks them up with what looks like one of its paws, and puts them into the basket.'

'Well, indeed, I never!' exclaimed Mrs Flittersnoop.

'Now,' said the Professor. 'Let us test out the machine. I have hidden one of my pairs of glasses and we shall see if the machine can find them.'

He adjusted a dial, pressed several buttons, and pulled a lever. The machine went trotting off into the kitchen.

'Is that where you hid your glasses?' asked Mrs Flittersnoop.

'I, er, really forget,' said the Professor.

'Well, I expect the machine will find them, wherever they are,' said Mrs Flittersnoop, more hopefully than she felt.

The machine pushed the kitchen door open and, making a noise like a rusty bark, came in with six wine glasses in its basket.

'Those aren't my spectacles!' said the Professor. 'I can't understand it. The machine has found something but not the right thing.'

'Glasses!' cried Mrs Flittersnoop. 'That's what it's found, sir, wine glasses not eye-glasses!'

'Um, ah yes, of course,' said the Professor. 'Some slight adjustment needed to the radioactive electronic detector coils.'

He fiddled about a bit and set the machine off again. This time it climbed upstairs with a lot of whizzing and clanking and came back with the hand mirror from Mrs Flittersnoop's dressing-table and the Professor's electrically-illuminated shaving mirror from the bathroom.

'Pah!' snorted the Professor. 'Looking glasses this time. Really, I spent so much time inventing this machine I think it ought to know the difference between eye-glasses and other kinds of glasses.'

In about two minutes he had the machine in bits all

over the floor, making adjustments here and alterations there, and changing circuits and replacing relays while Mrs Flittersnoop stood by wishing she hadn't cleaned the room as it was going to need cleaning again when the Professor had finished.

'Now, we'll try again,' said the Professor. He turned the dial, pressed the buttons and pulled the lever. Instantly the machine gave an excited yelp, shot outside, tore round the garden and came back with the Professor's missing fifth pair of spectacles in its basket, together with three thistles and part of a rosebush. The Professor had dropped his spectacles in the garden while trying to think of where to hide them, but that hadn't fooled the spectacle-finding machine.

'There now, well I never!' exclaimed Mrs Flittersnoop, feeling she ought to give the machine a lump of sugar.

'Success! Success!' cried the Professor, putting one of the thistles on his nose by mistake for the spectacles but discovering his mistake very quickly. 'We must try it again! Go and hide your sun-glasses somewhere, Mrs Flittersnoop, and we shall see if the machine can find them.'

Mrs Flittersnoop hid her sun-glasses in the linen cupboard under five pairs of sheets. The machine found them without pulling more than half the clean linen out with them. The Professor hid another pair of spectacles in his study and the machine located it at once, together with various pieces of wire the Professor had been using for an invention and which looked a bit like spectacles.

'Wonderful!' cried the Professor. He clapped the spectacles on, left the wire hanging round his ears and rushed off to see his friend Colonel Dedshott, to demonstrate the machine.

'Spectacles, by Jove!' cried Colonel Dedshott. 'My word, Branestawm, we can get it to bring the Naval and Military Tournament here from Olympia. That's a spectacle, all right. Save us buying seats and having to go there, what!'

But Commander Hardaport (Retired), who had been brought over to join in the excitement, said if it came to spectacles, the Naval Review off Spithead took precedence over a mere tournament. But, thank goodness, the Professor's machine wasn't equal to bringing all those battleships and half the North Sea into the Colonel's dining-room. Not that Commander Hardaport would have minded. He wasn't afraid of North Seas and he simply loved enormous battleships.

'But, look here, Branestawm!' said Colonel Dedshott. 'Rather a waste for your machine only to look for lost spectacles, isn't it?' The Colonel never wore spectacles, as he didn't consider them sufficiently military. 'It ought to be able to look for other things too.'

'Lost property locator, mark one,' said Commander Hardaport. 'Good idea, Dedshott! How about it, Professor?'

'Er, um, ah, why yes,' said the Professor, not feeling quite sure whether other people ought to be inventing his inventions for him. 'With a complex addition to the variability of the electronic detector valves, coupled to a more sophisticated type of dial, it could be managed, I think.'

In two and a half minutes the Colonel's sitting room was even more littered with bits of invention than the Professor's had been. But Colonel Dedshott didn't mind. His Catapult Cavalier butlers could soon be lined up and set to work clearing things up by numbers, which always gets things done much quicker, as the army will tell you.

'Good!' muttered the Professor as he got the machine together again with only a few parts left over. 'What shall we set it to look for?'

'Well, I've mislaid the medal I won for capturing five enemy sausage rolls during the battle of Snacker-plate,' said the Colonel. 'Can't find it anywhere!'

The Professor dialled *medal* and switched on the machine, which trotted into the Colonel's bedroom, tipped over the chest of drawers with a very military bang, scooped up the medal from where the Colonel had dropped it, brought it back and would have clicked its heels if it had had any.

'Wonderful, by Jove!' cried the Colonel.

'Ha!' cried Commander Hardaport. 'See if it can find my tin of binnacle polish. I haven't lost it, y'know, but see if your confounded machine can nose it out.'

The Professor spun the dial, pressed two buttons and pulled a lever. The machine sprang out of the window and vanished in the direction of the Commander's house, and was back with the tin of polish before the Commander could get his telescope focused on it.

'Marvellous!' cried the Colonel.

'I need never lose anything again!' cried the Professor with delight. 'The old story about the absent-minded Professors will have no meaning where I am concerned. My lost-property-locating machine has done away with all that.'

All three of them shook hands joyfully and nearly did away with a tray of coffee the Colonel's butlers had just brought in.

'Professor!' cried Mrs Flittersnoop from upstairs. 'Have you seen my new feather hat?'

'I can't look at it now, I'm in a hurry!' he called back.

'I mean, do you know where it is?' called Mrs Flittersnoop. 'I can't find it anywhere.'

'Don't worry!' said the Professor. 'The machine will find it for you.'

But just then the machine came in of its own accord, wearing the new feather hat which didn't suit it at all.

'Good gracious!' exclaimed the Professor. 'How did the machine know we wanted it to look for your hat? I never dialled it.'

But half an hour later the Professor couldn't find his shoes, had no idea where his handkerchiefs were and had mislaid several books. And Mrs Flittersnoop was hunting high and low for brushes and dustpans and saucepans and a tin marked *Rice* in which she kept sugar.

'It's that machine, I'll be bound!' she cried. And,

sure enough, in came the machine with its basket piled high with all the missing things which it tipped out on the floor.

'Dear, dear!' exclaimed the Professor. 'This is really most inconvenient.'

It certainly was. The Professor's marvellous lost property locator was getting a bit too efficient. Not enough things were getting lost, even in the Professor's house, to keep it busy. It had too much time on its cogwheels. So it was losing things on purpose so as to find them. Then it began losing things faster than it could find them again, because, of course, losing things is a great deal easier than finding them.

A plague of lost property broke out all over Great Pagwell as the Professor's machine set to work on his neighbours.

The Vicar was half way through a sermon when he discovered page 158 was missing, and he had to finish his sermon with funny stories. Dr Mumpzanmeazle lost his stethoscope, the Mayor lost his chain of office, Colonel Dedshott lost his sword and Commander Hardaport (Retired) lost his temper.

'Avast there!' he roared, rushing out into the garden waving a fish knife because he couldn't find the ex-naval cutlass he had intended to wave. 'Signal that machine of yours to heave to!' he shouted to the Professor across the fence. 'Can't have it taking people's property like this! Piracy on the high countryside, dammit!'

But the Professor didn't know what to do. He had lost the machine.

'Should I invent a machine to locate the lost property locator?' he muttered to himself. 'Or should I ring up the lost property office?'

He tried this, but the lost property office had to close because the Professor's machine had taken away all the lost property and distributed umbrellas, bird-cages, hockey-sticks, ladies' handbags, bicycles and false teeth to people all over Great Pagwell.

Colonel Dedshott collected some Catapult Cavaliers and began searching the streets. Commander Harda-port and Dr Mumpzanmeazle went around with a trawling net. And Pagwell Council dug up several miles of brand new drains in case the machine was hiding in them, but only succeeded in converting several one-way streets into no-way streets.

Soon there was a mass meeting in Great Pagwell Square to protest against things getting lost. Unfortu-nately it took place at the same time as another meeting protesting against protest meetings. And while the police were trying to sort out who was who, and why, the Professor's enthusiastic lost property locator came gal-loping down the main street.

Its basket was full to overflowing with everything you could think of and several things nobody would have thought of. It wore the Professor's five pairs of spectacles on one of its levers. The Mayor's chain was draped tastefully round its dial, and it was waving Dr Mupzanmeazle's stethoscope on top of its antennae. It rattled round the square, shedding lost property as it went.

'After it!' shouted Colonel Dedshott, pouncing on his sword. 'Come on, everyone!'

The crowd of protesters and anti-protestors joined forces and went swarming through the streets of Great Pagwell in pursuit of the machine.

It dodged down Sally Alley, doubled back up Flatt Hill, jumped a gate and was away across Farmer Plownough's fields.

'Hot pursuit!' roared Commander Hardaport, tearing along with three telescopes in one hand and a book of naval rules for dealing with pirates in the other.

'Head it off!' shouted Colonel Dedshott, feeling happier now he had his sword to wave.

Soon the whole population of Great Pagwell plus a few visitors, were streaming across Farmer Plownough's fields in pursuit of the machine.

'There it goes!' people shouted, pointing in different directions.

But it was no good. The machine had too good a start and Professor Branestawm's wonderful, amazing, too intelligent lost property locator mark one was lost for good, and never seen again.

Nobody knows where it went, but if you should lose something, don't worry too much. Perhaps one day there'll be a knock at the door and Professor Branestawm's machine will have found it for you.

2

Branestawm's Portable Car Park

PROFESSOR BRANESTAWM came out of Great Pagwell Town Hall to find a very large lady traffic warden standing by his car and glaring at it as if it was something the dustmen preferred not to take away. And it certainly looked as if it would resent being taken away by dustmen, being a special invention of the Professor's, with six wheels, two engines, a television set and a photo of the Mayor inside the bonnet.

'Are you driving this car?' she asked the Professor.

'Well, no, I'm not,' said the Professor.

'Then who is?' asked the traffic warden.

'Er, ah, nobody is driving it,' said the Professor, looking at the warden through various pairs of spectacles.

Car abandoned, wrote the traffic warden, in a fierce notebook. Then the Professor got into the car and started both engines.

'I thought you said this wasn't your car,' growled the traffic warden, crossing out what she'd written.

'Er, no, I didn't say that,' said the Professor. 'I said I was not driving it, but I am now going to do so.' He pulled a lever and the car slid sideways out of its parking space. He pressed a button and the car shot off down the street, while the traffic warden, who tried to clap a parking ticket on it, clapped it on the Mayor's car instead, which was parked just behind.

Of course, the Professor shouldn't have parked his car there at all because it was the space specially reserved for the Mayor's car. The Mayor had had to park his car behind, where there was a *No parking* notice, and so it really deserved the parking ticket the traffic warden awarded it. But she thought there might be a bit of a scandal if the Mayor was summonsed for parking outside his own Town Hall, and she tried to scrape the parking ticket off. And Pagwell's newest policeman nearly arrested her for trying to remove a parking ticket illegally.

'I shall have to do something about this car parking business,' said the Professor to Mrs Flittersnoop when he got home, too late for lunch and too early for tea. 'Wherever I go there are notices saying *No parking* and *No stopping* and *No entry* until really the only way to avoid breaking the law is to drive to where one wants to go, then drive straight home again without stopping and walk back.'

'You could take a bus, I suppose, sir,' said Mrs Flittersnoop, always willing to be helpful.

'There are severe penalties for taking buses or other municipal property,' said the Professor. 'And anyway, where could I park a bus if I can't park my car? No, I shall find a way of parking my car where I please without breaking the law. And I have an idea how I can do it.' He put on his hat and went out.

*

Professor Branestawm was on his way to Great Pagwell Library, when he came upon a large crowd of people.

'I'm afraid you'll have to go round another way,' said a policeman to the Professor. 'Someone's been knocked down by the library.'

'Have they really?' said the Professor. 'I had no idea libraries attacked people.' And he drove off down a side turning.

'I shall go to Pagwell Gardens Library,' said the Professor to himself. 'That's a nice quiet library.'

But, whether it was a nice quiet library or not, there was no space for the Professor to park his car and there were rows of traffic wardens brandishing parking tickets and waiting to pounce on him. So he went home again, arriving too late for tea and too early for supper.

'I'm going to Pagwell Gardens Library,' he said to Mrs Flittersnoop. 'And I shall go by train, which is much easier as one does not have to find anywhere to park a train.'

He got out of the train at Pagwell Gardens station and saw a large notice printed in British Rail's best black letters:

Passengers MUST cross the line by the footbridge, it said.

'Um,' said the Professor, and, as he was always careful to obey notices, he crossed the line by the footbridge.

When he got to the other side he was met by another notice, just like the first, saying, *Passengers MUST cross the line by the footbridge*.

'Well, I've just done that,' he said. 'But I suppose these British Rail people know best what is safe to do on a railway.' So he turned round and went back across the footbridge.

But when he got back there was the first notice, still saying that passengers MUST cross the line by the footbridge. It was quite firm about it.

'Oh dear, I am really afraid I shall have to disobey the rule,' muttered the Professor. He was just going to walk out of the station instead of crossing the line by the footbridge when Pagwell's newest policeman appeared.

'Now he's going to say, ''What's all this? Why aren't you crossing the line by the footbridge as the notice says?''' thought the Professor.

But the policeman said, 'Excuse me, sir, I'm new here. Can you direct me to the police station?'

'Certainly,' said the Professor, in his best law-abiding manner. 'Come this way, constable.' He walked straight past the footbridge notice and out into the streets of Pagwell Gardens, followed by the policeman.

'Take the first on the left and the third on the right,' said the Professor. 'And that will lead you to the police station.'

'Thank you very much, sir,' said the policeman. And off he went.

The Professor's directions didn't lead to the police station at all, but to the library. The Professor realized that he couldn't remember the way to the library himself and so he had to ask a passer-by who turned out to be a stranger to the place, and he directed the Professor to the police station instead of the library. But fortunately the Professor went the wrong way as usual and arrived at the library just as the new policeman he had misdirected to the police station arrived at the library as well.

Luckily there was a car parked the wrong way round in a *No parking* area during prohibited hours and obstructing the entrance to the car park. So that attracted the attention of the new policeman, and the Professor got into the library without any trouble, except from the revolving doors, which whizzed him round so that he kept coming out of the library instead of going into it.

But at last he was safely inside, and was asking for *The Bye-Laws, Rules and Regulations of the Rural Borough of Great Pagwell*. It told you all the things you mustn't do, and so it was a very thick book.

'Traffic Regulations,' said the Professor, turning the pages. 'Um, yes, here we are.'

The Great Pagwell Traffic Regulations included some from the Highway Code and some original ones of Great Pagwell's Council. They told you you mustn't park a car on the brow of a hill, at a bus stop, traffic lights or pedestrian crossing, alongside another vehicle or by road works. And they also told you, by courtesy of the Great Pagwell Council, that you could 'park a vehicle without charge in any approved car park in the Rural Borough of Great Pagwell' and it added very helpfully, 'A car park shall be any place where cars may be parked and such shall be designated by a notice inscribed *Car Park*.'

'Um, that seems clear enough,' said the Professor.

It was another day in Great Pagwell. And although it looked much the same as any day, this was an exceedingly special day.

For it was the day on which Professor Branestawm had decided to try out his wonderfully ingenious and incredibly simple 'Portable Car Park'.

'But you can't have a portable car park!' exploded Commander Hardaport (Retired) when the Professor told him about it. 'Car parks are whacking great pieces of ground! You can't go carrying them about.'

'I can carry my car park about,' said the Professor, and he set off for Great Pagwell to find somewhere to park his car in his portable car park.

He drew up in the High Street, opposite Ginnibag & Knitwoddle's Store. There were two yellow lines along the curb, and three policemen and two traffic wardens watching them.

The Professor stepped out of his car, raised his hat politely to the traffic wardens, who were ladies, but not to the policemen, who were not. Then he walked away.

'Excuse me sir!' 'Just a minute, please!' 'You can't do that here!' 'Come back!' shouted the policemen and the wardens like a grand opera chorus.

'Were you speaking to me?' asked the Professor, very politely.

'Yes, we were,' they said. 'You can't leave that car there. It's a *No parking* area.'

'Ah, pardon me,' said the Professor. 'But I have every right to park here. This is a car park,' and he pointed to a tall pole carrying a board that said in large capital letters CAR PARK.

'You just put that pole there yourself,' said one of the policemen.

'That doesn't make this a car park,' said one of the wardens, getting out a packet of parking tickets and several pencils.

'This,' said the Professor, waving spectacles about in the wind, '*is* the Rural Borough of Great Pagwell, I believe?'

'Of course it is,' said a policeman.

'Then my car is parked in an approved car park within the meaning of the bye-laws,' said the Professor, arranging his spectacles in a different order and smiling at the policeman.

'Nonsense, this is a prohibited area,' said the policeman. 'And you've no right to erect that pole neither.'

'A car park,' said the Professor, quoting the bye-laws very carefully as he had learnt them by heart, 'a car park shall be any place where cars may be parked and such shall be designated by a notice inscribed *Car Park*. And there is the notice,' finished the Professor, pointing triumphantly at his sign.

By this time five more cars, two delivery vans and a truck full of ironwork had parked themselves behind the Professor's car and his *Car Park* notice.

The three policemen and the two wardens stared in amazement.

'I think that has established my legal right to use my portable car park,' said the Professor. He got into his car and drove off, taking the pole with him, and immediately the two traffic wardens started joyfully giving out parking tickets to all the vehicles that had parked behind the Professor, while the policemen got into their police car and went whizzing off, with the horn going *bar*-bur, *bar*-bur, to catch the Professor.

Along Pagwell High Street shot the Professor. He came to a roundabout and drove on to it with the police car in hot and noisy pursuit. He turned off the round-

about, and found the road led into another roundabout. He turned off that and found himself in a third roundabout.

'Oh dear, this is worse than the footbridge at Pagwell Gardens Station,' he cried, going round and round the roundabout, not knowing where to turn off in case it took him into another roundabout. Then he saw a sign that said *City Centre*, and so he turned into that with the police car close behind him, and found himself back at the first roundabout.

'I shall never get out of this,' he murmured.

He turned left at the next exit but that took him back to the roundabout he had just come off.

'This is terrible!' he cried. 'I used to like going on roundabouts when I was little, but they were different. They had music, and horses . . . Good gracious! what's that?'

He had no sooner said the word 'music' than music broke out on the roundabout, and then horses appeared.

It was a detachment of the Catapult Cavaliers, with their band led by Colonel Dedshott, on their way to help the Mayor open a new hospital. The Professor had managed to get into the middle of a Municiple Procession. The police car, carefully giving way to vehicles already on the roundabout, finished up behind the Mayor's car and the policeman driver was watching so carefully to avoid running into the Mayor that he lost sight of the Professor.

Meanwhile the Professor had seen Colonel Dedshott. 'Dedshott!' he shouted. 'Help, Dedshott!'

'Hrrmp!' cried the Colonel. He yelled commands and stopped the horses and the band half-way round the roundabout. He didn't know whether there was a law saying that you mustn't stop a troop of horse soldiers with their band on a roundabout, but he wasn't going to leave his old friend Professor Branestawm in the lurch.

'My word, Branestawm, in trouble, what?' he shouted, cantering up to the Professor.

'I am afraid I have lost the way, Dedshott,' said the Professor.

'Ha!' grunted the Colonel. 'Follow us, Branestawm, soon have you out of this.'

He gave commands to the Catapult Cavaliers, and on they swept, out of one roundabout into the next, out of that and down the road that led past the hospital where the Mayor and his party were just arriving.

'Thank you very much, Dedshott,' called the Professor, very much relieved.

He drove past the hospital, down the street and parked his car outside Ye Olde Bunne Shoppe. There were five yellow lines painted along the curb, which meant nobody must ever leave a car within miles of the place, but the Professor just erected his portable car park sign beside his car and went in to have a quiet cup of tea and some fishpaste sandwiches to recover from his exhausting afternoon.

Meanwhile the policemen had also managed to escape from the Mayor's procession. They had gone off to call a meeting to see if they could get a law passed saying that nobody must park a car anywhere, not even in a car park, in case it happened to be Professor Branestawm's portable car park. And so large numbers of policemen and traffic wardens were driving around looking for somewhere to hold their meeting, when they saw a sign saying *Car Park* outside Ye Olde Bunne Shoppe, and decided that that would be a good place to go in case all that thinking made them hungry.

They parked their cars under what they thought was a genuine, hundred per cent, regulation car park sign, and everyone went in for tea and buns and thinking.

They had no sooner gone in than the Professor came out, full of tea and sandwiches and half a paper napkin he had eaten by mistake. And he took his car away together with his portable car park sign, leaving all the official cars illegally parked on yellow lines.

But, as usual, everything worked out for the best because when the policemen and traffic wardens came out, they got involved in such a complicated, legal argument as to whether they should give one another tickets for parking on yellow lines, that they forgot all about trying to arrest the Professor. And in the excitement of being rescued from the roundabouts by horses, the Professor had lost interest in his portable car park and had gone home to work on an even more shattering invention, a portable subway for making it safer to cross the road at roundabouts.

3

Professor Branestawm on the Scrap Heap

PAGWELL HARMONY was an extremely tidy and carefully ordered place. All the streets were quite straight and they didn't have names, they had numbers. All those going North and South were called Roads and were First Road, Second Road and so on. All those going East and West were Avenues, First Avenue, Second Avenue, etc. So it was almost impossible not to find your way unless you tried very hard and kept your eyes shut.

The traffic was controlled by special lights that said *Go* to the traffic and *Stop* to the people. Then they changed and said *Stop* to the traffic and *Run* to the people. A tremendous horn hooted and everybody tore across the street to get to the other side before the lights changed, and all the traffic had to wait for them to do it. So nobody was ever knocked down by a vehicle, although a lot of people were knocked down by one another.

The Town Council, of course, were the neatest of the neat. They all dressed exactly alike, all got to the office at the same moment, all went to lunch at exactly the same time, to the same place and had exactly the same to eat. The Town Clerk was so meticulous he always had the old letters put in strict alphabetical order before they were thrown away. If you ever dropped so much as a half a piece of paper on the ground, special anti-litter policemen swooped down on you, picked you up and put you in a little prison that looked like a dustbin where you had to stay until you promised never to do it again. And the dustmen called twice a day to make sure not the least bit of rubbish remained uncollected.

But the most remarkable thing of all about Pagwell Harmony was the place where all the rubbish, empty tins and bottles, bits of old iron and scrap metal, dis-carded bicycles and broken-down motor cars were taken. These were carefully sorted out and the burnable things were burnt. The others were neatly stacked in heaps of different kinds. The old motor cars were lined up with disused tractors and discarded railway engines and unwanted steamrollers. And people could go along and buy them. You simply unscrewed whatever bit you wanted, took it to the office and paid for it.

Professor Branestawm didn't know anything about this, until he came on it by accident. He was going to Pagwell-over-Poppington, when he lost the way and arrived in Pagwell Harmony by mistake. The first part of it he saw was the neat and tidy Refuse Depository.

'Well, good gracious me!' he exclaimed. 'This is really wonderful! Why it's just the place I would have been looking for if I had had any idea it existed, which I hadn't!' He looked at all the lovely heaps of sorted oddments of everything through all his five pairs of spectacles. 'There is material here for a million inventions,' he gasped. 'I can find anything I want here and a great deal more. Dear, dear, how very fortunate!'

The Professor was in such a state of excitement that he rushed round wondering what to buy and what to invent it into. But he was so excited he couldn't think at all. He felt as if he had indigestion inside his head. His brains whizzed.

'Dear me!' he muttered. 'I really must calm myself. I had better go away and decide what I want to invent, then come back another day and choose what I want nice and calmly.' And off he shot to tell Colonel Dedshott about this wonderful island of uninvented inventions he had discovered.

'You must come with me, Dedshott,' he said. 'We will borrow a cart and your horse shall take us in it, and then we shall have plenty of, um, ah, transport to bring back all the things I shall want.'

'By Jove, Branestawm!' snorted Colonel Dedshott. 'A treasure house of, er, er, whatsname, my word! But a horse and cart won't be good enough, you know. I shall get the army to lend us something more adequate.'

What the army finally lent him was a rather dented tank they had used for warlike exercises. But it didn't have an engine, and so Colonel Dedshott's horse was harnessed to it, accompanied by three other Catapult Cavalier horses, as the tank was too heavy for one to pull.

As they clopped and clanked through the streets of Great, Upper, North and Little Pagwell, some of the people thought they were part of a military tattoo, others thought they were advertising a new kind of cleaner for saucepans, and others didn't think anything at all because they were too busy wondering what the country was coming to.

'Here we are, Dedshott!' cried the Professor excitedly as they arrived at the Scrap and Refuse Depository.

Colonel Dedshott reined in the four horses, which was four times as difficult as reining in his one horse, and the Professor was half way to a heap of cogwheels almost before they had stopped.

'Better turn the horses loose to graze,' muttered the Colonel. 'No sense in keeping them tied up.'

Professor Branestawm was already collecting inventing materials like a bee collecting honey. He scooped up scrap metal, he pounced on pieces of plastic, he grabbed gas-fittings, and Colonel Dedshott, ever helpful, followed him about with boxes to put the stuff in.

'Er, ah, puff, puff,' panted the Professor after a while. 'This is really rather tiring, Dedshott. I suggest we stop for lunch.'

'Ha, yes, jolly good idea!' said the Colonel, putting down a box of old iron.

They settled down between the bedsteads and the cogwheels, where they had a nice view of some steam-rollers and a pile of cream cartons. They had a good lunch that Mrs Flittersnoop had packed for them, and of course there was no problem of leaving litter because they were in the very place where you were supposed to leave litter.

Then on they went with the collecting until at last
the Professor had as much as he thought they could get
into the tank. So they queued up with all the other
people who were buying junk, to pay for it.

'Look at that!' said Colonel Dedshott, pointing to a
piece of metal someone else was carrying. 'Just like one
of the things on our tank, by Jove!'

'And he's picked up a piece of piping that might also
be a gun from a tank,' said the Professor.

But none of the junk buyers had anything like as
much as the Professor and Colonel, and they had to
get some of the Refuse Depository men to help them
carry it back to their tank.

'Um, ah, where did we leave the tank?' said the
Professor, looking round but not seeing it.

'It can't be far away,' said the Colonel, collecting
the horses together and giving them lumps of sugar
Mrs Flittersnoop had kindly provided, she being rather
fond of animals.

'What did you say you brought to take the stuff
away?' asked one of the Refuse Depository men.

'A practice target tank used for manoeuvres,' said the
Colonel. 'A bit dented, you know, but pretty good, by
Jove.'

'Dear, dear!' said the Depository man. 'You know,
I'm very much afraid some of our customers thought
your tank was one of the discarded things for taking to
pieces and buying.'

'What!' roared the Colonel, stamping his feet till
his spurs jingled like alarm clocks. 'Arrest them! Steal-

ing government property! Absconding with military material! Shot at dawn, by Jove! After them.'

He lept on two horses at once and tried to dash off in pursuit of anybody in sight, but the Refuse man grabbed the reins.

'No, no, Colonel!' he cried. 'You can't do that. They thought the tank was here to be dismantled and bought. You can't blame them. You really shouldn't have left it unattended, you know. People are so careless. Why, only last week the Mayor of Pagwell Gardens thought-lessly left his car here while he bought a bicycle wheel for his nephew, and lost his rear bumper.'

So there was nothing they could do. The Refuse men sold them, nice and cheap, the bottom part of a traction engine on which they stacked the boxes of stuff they had collected. Then they harnessed the horses to it and drove home. And all the way home some people thought they were a new kind of rag and bone men, and some thought they were advertising a circus, and some thought they were doing it for the films, but others still thought they didn't know what the country was coming to.

When General Shatterfortz heard about his lovely practice tank being taken apart and bought by do-it-yourself people he blew up like ten batteries of enormous guns all going off at once. And some of the rather nervous Catapult Cavaliers who were just going on parade went back to bed and pretended to be ill, while others tried to leave the Catapult Cavaliers and join the submarines because they thought it would be safer.

'My word, Branestawm!' gasped Colonel Dedshott when at last he could get away from the exploding General. 'You nearly had me court martialled, by Jove! Almost had me shot at dawn for the second time. Pretty well had me drummed out of the army, dammit! The only thing that saved me was the shortage of soldiers. Lack of Colonels, y'know.'

'Dear me,' said the Professor. 'I am most awfully sorry. I really didn't realize that my collecting odds and ends for inventions could cause so much trouble in the army.' Then suddenly the Professor had an idea. 'I know what to do. I'll *invent* a tank to replace the one we lost. Just what I need to use some of the things we've collected.'

'Yes, by Jove!' cried the Colonel. 'Specially deadly tank invented by Professor Branestawm puts British Army ahead of all other nations. That'll please the General! Put me in the clear. Might even get me promoted to whatever comes next to Colonel which I ought to know, but can't remember.'

'Come, Dedshott. No time to lose,' cried the Professor He grabbed the Colonel, rushed him into his inventory and started inventing full speed ahead and all valves open.

For days and nights inventing noises came rumbling out of the Professor's inventory. Mrs Flittersnoop invented several kinds of astonishing meals that the Professor could eat without using his hands as they were both occupied with inventing. Colonel Dedshott managed to get off from several vital parades so as to be at hand with military advice.

At last the miraculous military tank was finished. It was the tank to end all tanks. It was the answer to every enemy army in the world.

'This will be such an overwhelming threat to other countries, Dedshott,' said the Professor, waving arms and spectacles and bits of old iron about, 'that nobody will dare to attack anyone. It will abolish war.'

'By Jove, I hope not!' grunted the Colonel. 'Lose my job if it does, dammit!'

But the Colonel didn't really believe the Professor's invention would abolish war and armies, because he knew the Professor's inventions were always a bit unexpected.

And this new truculent military tank was as unexpected as anything could be.

It had fifteen guns of different sizes and lengths including one tremendous boss of a gun that could extend in sections like a telescope so as to blow the enemy to bits at close quarters without the tank coming within range of the enemy's guns. It had quick-firing guns that fired more shots to the second than anyone could count and had a special computer to count them. It had anti-aircraft guns firing straight up in the air and anti-submarine guns firing straight into the ground. The tank could act as a battleship when required, and it had mine detectors and flame throwers and bomb hurlers and gas belchers and a special attachment for cutting the braces of the enemy troops so that their trousers would fall down and they couldn't even run away.

The entire force of Catapult Cavaliers was drawn up in tattoo-watching order to see the demonstration of Professor Branestawm's new, frightful and undefeatable tank. The War Office sent down several highly-placed gentlemen in special bowler hats. The Mayor and Councillors of Great Pagwell were lined up in a special box draped with Union Jacks, and Mrs Flittersnoop, Dr Mumpzanmeazle, the vicar and Commander Hardaport (Retired) were in viewing positions up trees, on top of buses or at friends' windows, according to whom they knew.

General Shatterfortz, smothered in medals and with his whiskers screwed up extra tight, gave the order for the demonstration to start. The Catapult Cavaliers trumpeters sounded a fanfare and the Professor's tank came trundling on to the field like a huge tin duck.

It drew up in front of the General, and fired a rapid salute of forty-five guns. Then it swung round to face the enemy, which consisted of a row of soldiers cut out of plywood.

Boom! Bang! Rat-a-tat-tat-tat! went the tank's guns and the wooden soldiers went up in sawdust and smoke.

'Bravo, Branestawm!' shouted Commander Hardaport from his tree-top which was the nearest he could get to being up the mast of a ship.

Then the Catapult Cavaliers opened fire on the tank with ten field guns.

Bong! Bong! Bong! Bong!

The tank shot out its guns, fired them all at once and smothered everywhere in dark green smoke that smelt of burnt shepherd's pie and cough lozenges.

'Hurray for the Professor!' shouted the Vicar and Dr Mumpzanmeazle.

'Very good indeed, I'm sure, sir!' said Mrs Flitter-snoop, who was on top of a bus driven by sister Aggie's second cousin, Alf. But then the bus had to move on and she didn't see the rest of the show.

The tank proceeded to dig itself into the ground, let off a few shots at imaginary aeroplanes and came out again to face an attack by Catapult Cavaliers flame throwers. The flames engulfed the Professor's tank but it covered itself with ice and squirted water at the flame throwers which sizzled and stopped flame throwing.

Then some unauthorized person threw a pot of home-made marmalade at the tank. It burst on top and marmalade trickled through cracks.

'Tut, tut, this is very irregular!' grunted the Professor, working levers in a remote control cabin at the end of the field. 'If they, er, gum up the works, I fear there may be trouble.'

There was.

The Professor's tank was quite happy dealing with soldiers and guns and bombs and flame throwers. But marmalade was more than it expected. The computer-operated mechanism didn't respond to the Professor's remote control. The tank swung round and shot half the General's medals off, then it went clanking round the field firing purple smoke and marmalade at the Catapult Cavaliers. It dug itself into the ground, tunnelled under the Pagwell Councillors' viewing box and came up in the middle of the Officers' tennis court.

'After it!' roared Colonel Dedshott, drawing his sword and cutting down a string of flags.

'Stop that tank at once!' roared the General. 'The tennis court must be saved at all costs.'

The tank was playing itself at tennis, lobbing grenades over the net.

The Professor frantically pushed and pulled all the levers.

The tank rose into the air, came back over the field and sprayed the troops with rubber bullets coated with marmalade.

'Open fire with anti-aircraft guns!' roared the General.

The War Office gentlemen hurriedly wrote notes in triplicate and concealed them in their bowler hats. The Professor stamped on ten different buttons.

The tank came apart into sixteen little tanks, and the Professor jumped on the remote control box. The little tanks piled themselves up in a heap and caught fire. The Pagwell Fire Brigade came rushing up and put the fire out, and then the refuse collecting department of Pagwell Harmony arrived and carted the bits away to the Refuse Depository, where they were neatly sorted out into heaps of cogwheels and levers and bits of this and that ready for people to buy for making other things out of.

So the scrap went eventually to the scrap heap and the Professor's latest invention was carefully and tidily returned to where it all started.

'Well, it does save having to clean the place up,' said Mrs Flittersnoop. And she went into the kitchen to get on with the ironing while Professor Branestawm turned his attention to inventing an invention for inventing inventions.

4

The Pipes of Pandemonium

'It isn't as loud this time,' said Mrs Flittersnoop.

'No,' said the Professor, 'but it's going on longer.'

'But not as long as last Thursday,' said Mrs Flittersnoop.

'Friday mornings are the worst,' said the Professor. 'We shall have to get something done about it.' He gathered up his five pairs of spectacles and went into his study, dropping three of them into the waste paper basket.

They had been talking about water pipe noises.

'I do hope we aren't going to have all that trouble we had some time ago,' said Mrs Flittersnoop, following him into his study and fishing the spectacles out of the waste paper basket. 'The noise was so awful we couldn't sleep for it, and then when it stopped we couldn't sleep without it because we'd got so used to it.'

'Ah yes,' said the Professor, 'I remember. I had to invent a noise-making machine so that we could sleep, and gradually make it less and less noisy. But I'm not going to do that again. I shall call in the plumbers.'

'You aren't going to have a try at it yourself first?' asked Mrs Flittersnoop, hoping that he wasn't.

But she needn't have worried, because the Professor

was still deep in special inventions for car parks that you could put in subways under roundabouts, and thus park your car and cross the road at the same time.

He wrote to some plumbers that he knew and asked them to come and deal with the pipes. They came, two of them, a short, jolly little man in a cap and a very young man with a lot of hair.

'The pipes go *weeeeee* when the hot tap is turned on,' said the Professor.

'And they go *zim, zim, zim, zim*, when the cold tap is turned off,' added Mrs Flittersnoop.

'If the hot tap is turned off very slowly,' said the Professor, 'the noise goes on, and if the cold tap is turned on very suddenly, the noise then stops. But if both taps are turned on at once and then turned off separately, the noise stops, then goes on again, until the hot water tap is turned on and the cold tap is turned on and then off, and then the noises stop, start again and stop. Unless of course the cold tap is turned on first and both taps are turned off together.'

'Ah!' said long hair.

'You gotta be re-piped,' said the jolly man, grinning like a Prime Minister.

'I gotta be what did you say?' asked the Professor, thinking his ears weren't working properly.

'Re-piped, guv,' said the jolly man. 'Them noises what your pipes are making, now that we can stop. That's just a hair lock.'

'A hair lock?' said the Professor. 'How can a lock of hair be responsible for all that noise?'

'Not an *air* lock, a *hair* lock,' said the jolly man.

'I think he means air lock,' said Mrs Flittersnoop, trying to be helpful.

'Yes, a hair lock in them pipes,' said the jolly man. 'We can sort that out easy, but all these water pipes are proper wore out, guv, and that's a fact.'

He reached under the sink, and pulled out a length of pipe which crumbled up in his hands.

'See what I mean!' said the jolly man.

'Um,' said long hair, taking half a cigarette from behind his left ear, looking at it and putting it behind his right ear.

'Oh dear, oh dear!' cried Mrs Flittersnoop. 'That sounds awful! Do you mean we must have all the water pipes taken out and new ones put in?'

'Throughout,' said the jolly man. 'Otherwise you'll get trouble.'

'We already have trouble,' said the Professor. 'We have trouble with the pipes making noises. Do I understand you to say that we must now have more trouble in order to get rid of the trouble we already have?'

'Well, it's like this, guv,' said the jolly man, popping a peppermint into his mouth and rattling it round his teeth. 'If we don't re-pipe you, the pipes what are rotten are liable to break up, and then where are you?'

'I'm 'ere,' said long hair.

'Not you!' said the jolly man. 'I mean to say, guv, you could be flooded out proper.'

'How long will it take to, um, ah, re-pipe us?' asked the Professor.

'Well, not more'n two weeks, that is to say, two working weeks, which, as we only work five days a week and a full week is seven days, means fourteen days' work,' said the jolly man. 'And that comes out at about three weeks, give or take a few days. On the other hand, it might just take a couple of hours. You never can tell.'

'But we can't be without water for three weeks!' gasped Mrs Flittersnoop, thinking of all the washing she couldn't do. 'We should run out of the Professor's pyjamas!'

'Ah now, Mrs Flittersnoop,' said the Professor. 'You could go and stay with your sister Aggie I have no doubt.'

'Well, yes, indeed, I'm sure, sir, I could do that,' said Mrs Flittersnoop. 'But what about you?'

'I have an idea that this would be a good opportunity to go and stay with some friends of mine in Pagwell Gardens Suburb who asked me to visit them,' said the Professor.

So the jolly man and long hair were told to get on with the re-piping, and Professor Branestawm went to stay with Mr and Mrs Horace Hokkibats. They were a very sporting couple he had met at a lecture on table tennis in its relation to ludo under the continental influence of Italian basket-ball, which he had once attended by mistake.

Mr Hokkibats was a tall, skinny gentleman with square spectacles. He was a part-time sports commentator with the Pagwell Broadcasting Company, because

he could talk extremely quickly and describe games even faster than people could play them. In fact, when he was commentating on a football game, the players had a hard job keeping up with him. The match of the year between Pagwell United and Pagwell Friday resulted in a score of Pagwell United 2, Pagwell Friday 3, and Horace Hokkibats 7.

Mrs Hetty Hokkibats, who was a retired games

teacher, was small, round and bouncy, like a tennis ball. Both of them loved games of all kinds, and their house was rather like Wimbledon, Lords, Henley and the Imperial Chess Club, all in one building.

'I'm sure you'll find plenty to amuse you here, Professor,' said Hetty Hokkibats, lobbing the Professor's hat on to a netball goal in the hall. 'We are great believers in making life a game.'

'Rather!' said her husband. 'Well, we had better make an ascent on your room right away. Breakfast kick-off at eight thirty tomorrow.'

He carried the Professor's suitcase up the stairs with great difficulty, partly because the Professor had packed quantities of inventing tools in his with clothes, which made the case very heavy, and partly because the staircase was laid out as a bowling alley, where you bowled up the stairs at some skittles arranged on the first landing and your ball was returned down a shute at the side of the stairs.

'I hope you slept well, Professor,' said Mrs Hokkibats, next morning.

'I, um, er, that is to say,' mumbled the Professor. In fact, he had hardly slept at all because the ceiling of his bedroom was marked out as a chess problem, and he had been trying to work it out all night. In addition the bed was made like a dodgem car, and kept sliding round the room, bumping off the furniture. He had finally managed to get a little sleep by sitting in the wardrobe.

Mrs Hokkibats blew a sharp blast on a whistle, and Mr Hokkibats, who had been limbering up on the lawn, came running into the dining room and breakfast began.

'And it's bacon coming down on the left side, closely followed by fried eggs, but dry toast looks like overtaking if the kippers don't catch them at the first fork,' jabbered Mr Hokkibats, as Mrs Hokkibats dealt plates of breakfast round like playing cards in a mad game of whist.

The dining table was a tennis table, so that you had to pass the salt and pepper and marmalade over the net. If you missed it, that counted against you, and you lost half an egg or a piece of toast.

'It's all over with the porridge, and the rice crispies are well down!' shrieked Hector. 'Now it's two to one the boiled eggs get cracked and don't make the cup.'

Mrs Hokkibats neatly fielded a grilled kidney and sent the Professor down a fast leg-break sausage. The Professor, who rarely remembered to eat any breakfast anyway, would not even have tried now, except that Mrs Hokkibats failed to return the toast her husband had sent over in a half volley so that it landed on the Professor's plate and he ate it almost in his sleep.

'Well, we're coming to the end of another exiting breakfast!' said Mr Hokkibats, 'and it looks as though Mrs Hokkibats will shortly be relegated to the washing up. In the meanwhile, Professor, I suggest I show you round our house.'

They looked at the bathroom, which had an enormous dartboard on the wall where you had to score double top before you could have a bath. The drawing room was papered with crossword puzzles, which you had to rub out as soon as you had done them so that they would be ready for the next person to attempt. There was clock golf in the hall, where you had to stand inside the grandfather clock and try to get the ball into the umbrella stand at the far end.

All the time they were looking Mr Hokkibats kept up a running commentary that would have won the eight million metres in the Olympic Games, explaining it all to the Professor, who couldn't listen fast enough.

'Um, most remarkable,' he said, wondering how he could invent some way of getting out of the place without first having to throw a double six with dice, or draw the ace of hearts from a pack of cards.

By the end of the afternoon, the Professor, tired out by playing games he didn't understand, decided to ring up his house to see how the re-piping was going. But somehow he managed to dial the wrong number, and when he thought he was connected to his own house, he had really got the Great Pagwell School of Scottish Music instead.

'Have you done the pipes at my house yet?' he asked, not realizing that anything was wrong.

'Is it pipes ye're wanting, then?' said a very Scottish lady at the other end. 'Weel, it isna hogmanay nor Robbie Burrrrns' birthday, ye ken, but if it's the pipes ye're wanting we'll no be stopping ye.'

'No, no, I'm Professor Branestawm,' protested the Professor. 'It's at my house, the pipes. Is everything in, um, ah, order?'

'Aye, I've got yer order, Professor, never fear,' said the Scottish lady. 'We'll be away and see it to the noo.'

She rang off, still thinking the Professor wanted bagpipes played at his home. And, with true Scottish efficiency, the Great Pagwell School of Scottish Music sent plenty of pipers and a' and a' round to the Professor's house.

Meanwhile Colonel Dedshott had decided to go and visit Professor Branestawm at the Hokkibats household. 'May be glad of a chat with no inventing to do. Probably a bit bored by now, what!' He mounted his horse and rode off.

Mr and Mrs Hokkibats welcomed him with open arms, and before he knew where he was the Colonel was involved in a complicated game of tennis on horseback, which he found rather difficult because his horse kept tripping over the croquet hoops on the tennis court.

Professor Branestawm saw his chance. He grabbed a bicycle belonging to Mr Hokkibats and set off for home as fast as he could, which wasn't very fast because the bicycle was a special one made for cycle racing in the drawing room and no matter how hard you pedalled it barely moved.

'This is awful!' groaned the Professor. 'It would be quicker to walk.' He leant the bicycle against a lamppost, and started walking. Then he found it would be even quicker to run and quicker still to take a bus.

At last he arrived at his house.

'Oh, no, this is worse than ever!' he cried.

The plumbers had gone, it was true. But the noise was worse than before.

Weeeee! Owowowowowowo!

'I won't have it!' cried the Professor. 'I shall ring up the water company and complain about the plumbers.'

But of course it wasn't the plumbers' fault the noises were worse than ever. In every room of the Professor's house there were enormous persons in kilt, sporran, tartan and skene-dhu (which is a sort of Scottish flick knife used for stabbing wild haggis). And they were playing the bagpipes for all they were worth, which was a good deal, because Scottish people are very careful with their money.

Weee! Zooooom! Weee!

And, because they were all in different rooms, stamping up and down as bagpipers have to, they couldn't hear what the others were playing. So they were all playing different tunes. And the mixture of *Flowers of the Forest* and *Scotland the Brave* and various other laments, marches and reels certainly sounded much worse than the water pipe noise.

'Stop this noise at once! I want to telephone!' shouted the Professor to the piper in the dining room.

'What's that?' said the piper.

'I want to telephone!' shouted the Professor.

'I canna hear ye for these damn pipes!' shouted the piper.

The Professor rushed upstairs.

'Yon's a queer mon,' said the piper to himself. 'He doesna like the pipes.'

He went out into the garden, where he ran into Colonel Dedshott, who had managed to get away from the Hokkibatses at last by jumping over the tennis net on his horse and galloping off.

'My word, what's all this, by Jove?' he was saying, as he got off his horse.

'The Professor doesna like the pipes,' said the piper.

'My word, no I should think not!' said the Colonel. 'If the water pipes in my house made that row I'd have something to say, I can tell you!'

He stamped into the house to look for the Professor and found him sitting on the floor at the foot of the stairs, shouting at the telephone.

'But we've stopped the noises, guv,' said the jolly man at the other end of the phone, because the Professor had got on to the plumbers instead of the water company, which he was trying to telephone. 'We got rid of that hair lock, and everything's nice and quiet, you'll find.'

'*Quiet?*' yelled the Professor.

Colonel Dedshott stumped up the stairs shouting military commands. Commander Hardaport, the Professor's next door neighbour, came in shouting complaints, because the only kind of pipe he liked was a Bosun's pipe. And the noise was worse than ever.

But fortunately at that moment Mrs Flittersnoop came back from her sister Aggie's and made tea and shortbread for the pipers. As soon as they noticed this they stopped piping immediately. Two very agile pipers did a sword dance on fish knives in the garden, for a lark. Colonel Dedshott exchanged English and Scottish military stories with the chief piper, who was very high up in a Highland regiment. And Commander Hardaport (Retired) told tall sea stories to the other pipers, who were also tall.

And the Professor sank into a chair, and said, 'Well, thank goodness that's over, whatever it was! And thank goodness the water pipe noises are finished with.'

But just then a wailing and gurgling broke out overhead as Mrs Flittersnoop turned the cold tap off rather quickly after re-filling the tea kettle.

'Stop it!' shouted the Professor. 'I will *not* have it! Fetch the plumbers! Call the water company!'

But it wasn't necessary to call any of these distinguished people. The chief piper, who was used to climbing about in the Highlands, climbed to the roof and found that what was causing the noises hadn't been the fault of the water pipes at all. It was an old invention of the Professor's for protecting the house against being struck by lightning. He had put it up in the roof and connected it to the water pipes for safety. And it made lightning-conducting noises which the water pipes transmitted right through the house.

That left the Professor to decide whether it was better to be protected against being struck by lightning during a storm than to be struck by water pipe noises all the time, unless you remembered to turn the hot water on first or the cold water off first, or to turn them off slowly or suddenly according to which you had turned on or off first.

5

Mrs Flittersnoop's Birthday Present

MRS FLITTERSNOOP had a birthday coming on. And, goodness gracious, Professor Branestawm knew about it!

'Ah, Mrs Flittersnoop,' he said heartily, at breakfast. 'I believe next Tuesday is your birthday?'

Goodness knows how the Professor managed to remember that, as he certainly never remembered his own birthday, or how old he was, and very often he didn't remember where he lived. But Mrs Flittersnoop's sister Aggie had sent him a large secret letter reminding him of the date so that may have had something to do with it.

'I wonder,' went on the Professor, 'whether you would let me know what you would, er, like for a present.'

'Well, indeed, that's very kind, I'm sure, sir,' said Mrs Flittersnoop, thinking away like mad about what she would like to have that the Professor might possibly manage to buy without getting it too wrong.

'I think perhaps you might, ah, mark something you would like in this catalogue of Ginnibag & Knitwoddle's,' said the Professor.

That was an idea of sister Aggie's, too. The Professor

handed over the Pagwell telephone directory in mistake for the catalogue.

'Thank you very much, sir,' said Mrs Flittersnoop, taking the telephone directory with the air of the Mayoress receiving an illuminated address. But she put it away and got out the catalogue instead, because she didn't really want the Great Pagwell Fire Station for a birthday present, or the second-hand bicycle shop in Lower Pagwell.

'Now, what shall I choose?' she murmured, when the breakfast was cleared away and the Professor was safely stowed in his inventory, happily clashing things about. 'I could do with a new hat,' she said to herself turning the pages of the catalogue and watching the new hats flash by. Naturally no lady ever has enough new hats. But hats are a little on the tricky side. For one thing you can't be happy in a hat unless it's really you, and Mrs Flittersnoop didn't think Professor Branestawm would know at sight whether a hat was really her or not. And anyway, with another birthday coming on, she was reaching a slightly risky age where hats were concerned, having got past the time when she was afraid a hat was too old for her, which would have been awful, and now rather worried in case a hat should be too young for her which would be just as bad.

'Or again,' she said to herself, 'a pair of warm gloves would be nice, or perhaps some scent.' She giggled a bit at the thought of the Professor giving her an exotic flask of *Temptation of Eve* or *Venus Passion*.

Finally she settled for a nice new handbag, not too

expensive, and big enough to take all the used bus tickets, out-of-date timetables, face tissues, packets of peppermints, nail scissors, nail files, lipstick, pencils, spare buttons, reels of cotton, safety pins, shopping lists, holiday snapshots, raffle tickets, and handbills of steamer trips which she might need to carry with her.

'That will be lovely!' she said to herself, and she made a nice thick cross against the handbag and put the catalogue on the Professor's desk.

'Ah, what's this?' mumbled the Professor, finding the catalogue. 'Ginnibag & Knitwoddle's catalogue! Dear me, did I order something from them and if so what was it? Some new screw drivers with self ejecting ends? A set of heavy hammers? No, no, they don't sell things like that.' He turned over the pages and came on a page with something marked with a big cross.

'Ha!' he exclaimed, clapping his hand to his head and scattering his spectacles all over the carpet. 'Yes, yes, of course, fancy me forgetting! This is what Mrs Flittersnoop wants for her birthday. Let me see. Good gracious!'

No wonder the Professor was astonished. The mark was placed against an elegant pipe rack, complete with a device for cleaning pipes, including a bowl scraper-out, a stem pusher-through and a tobacco shover-down.

'I really had no idea Mrs Flittersnoop smoked a pipe,' he said, 'but you never can tell these days.' And he went off to buy Mrs Flittersnoop a very special pipe rack that she certainly didn't want.

Well then, why had she marked it in the catalogue? Was she getting as absent-minded as the Professor? No, in fact she hadn't marked the pipe rack at all. She had made such a heavy inky cross against the handbag she wanted that the ink had gone right through the paper and marked itself against the pipe rack that was on the other side of the page. But how was the Professor to know that?

The Professor was looking at the pipe rack in his inventory, out of the way so that Mrs Flittersnoop shouldn't see it and spoil the surprise. 'Not that it could be much of a surprise,' he thought, 'as she already knows what I'm giving her.' Which just shows that things were not a bit as he thought, but then they hardly ever were with the Professor.

'I wonder what Mrs Flittersnoop can possibly want with this pipe rack?' he said to himself. He turned it over and round and round. He examined the pipe cleaning device. 'Perhaps she wants to use it for something else,' he thought. 'I know she uses an old coffee tin to put the milkman's money in and keeps an old knife with no handle to open tight lids. Yes, yes, that would be it. But I wonder what she is going to use this for?'

He started to think. And once Professor Branestawm started to think you never knew what it would lead to. In about ten minutes he had thought of fifteen different things he could use the pipe rack for and by tea time he had taken it to bits and invented it into several unlikely pieces of machinery.

Of course that put Mrs Flittersnoop's birthday clean out of his mind. And, when next Tuesday arrived there he was on Mrs Flittersnoop's birthday morning with no present to give her except a novelty pipe rack that was in all bits.

'Good morning, sir,' said Mrs Flittersnoop, putting a sausage in front of him.

'Ah, good morning, Mrs Flittersnoop,' said the Professor. Then he noticed a parcel beside his plate.

'Dear, dear, is it my birthday already?' he muttered.

He looked at the parcel and found a label on it that said, *To Mrs Flittersnoop, with birthday wishes from Professor Branestawm.*

Mrs Flittersnoop, who knew enough about the Professor to guess that he would never have managed to get her a present without getting himself in a muddle, had bought the handbag on his behalf. And she had gift-wrapped it for herself, too, so that all the Professor had to do was hand it graciously over with birthday remarks and plenty of smiles. And this he did without any trouble.

'Oh, thank you very much, I'm sure, sir,' she said. She unwrapped the parcel, folded the paper neatly, and said, 'A handbag! How lovely! Just what I wanted. It is most kind of you to remember my birthday, indeed, I'm sure, sir.'

And she helped him to another sausage.

6

Branestawm's Labour-Saving Christmas

'I THINK we'll have the golden angels across here,' said the Vicar of Pagwell, clinging to the top of a shaky ladder in Pagwell Church Hall and not feeling nearly as happy to be that much nearer heaven as he thought he ought to.

'I don't think there are quite enough to reach,' said Dr Mumpzanmeazle, who was giving a hand decorating the hall for Christmas. 'How about interspersing them with these birdcage affairs?'

'Oh, I don't really think so, sir!' put in Mrs Flitter-snoop, who, with her sister Aggie from Lower Pagwell and a few extra friends, was making herself useful. 'I mean to say, it might look as if the angels had escaped from the cages, don't you think so, Vicar?'

The discussion was interrupted at this moment by a series of sharp commands outside and a great deal of stamping of horses' hoofs and jingling of harness, and a moment later in marched Colonel Dedshott at the head of five Catapult Cavaliers in working dress, which meant no medals, very short haircuts and second best boots.

'Ha! There you are, Vicar!' cried the Colonel, saluting reverently. 'Thought you'd like some help putting up the decorations, so here we are!' He waved towards the Catapult Cavaliers and knocked a box of coloured glass balls out of Mrs Flittersnoop's hands, but fortunately they were instantly saved by the Catapult Cavaliers who played cricket a lot and were good at catching.

'That's extremely kind of you, my dear Colonel,' said the Vicar. 'I'm afraid this Christmas decoration business is rather, that is to say, somewhat of a . . .'

'Ruddy nuisance!' said the Mayor, coming in at that moment. 'I ordered three dozen assorted floral garlands for you, Vicar, and Ginnibag & Knitwoddle haven't sent them.'

'Never mind,' said Dr Mumpzanmeazle, being very practical. 'Now you're here, Mayor, you can give a hand with these paper chains.'

But the Mayor, who was used to wearing an elegant gold chain, wasn't used to fragile paper chains, and had soon got himself tied up in quantities of crinkly paper.

'Oh dear, oh dear!' sighed Mrs Flittersnoop. 'We shall never get the hall decorated if these gentlemen keep coming in to help. Many hands make light work, but what I say is too many cooks spoil the broth, which, thank goodness, there isn't any of here at present or I'm sure it would get spilt and have to be cried over.'

The work of decorating the hall went on like this for some time, until Mrs Flittersnoop and sister Aggie retired to a little side room to put kettles on and prepare refreshments for the tired decorators. The Vicar came carefully down the ladder, followed by the angels, which he hadn't tied up securely enough. Dr Mumpz-anmeazle was called away to someone suffering from an overdose of mince pies, and Colonel Dedshott, not knowing what to order his Cavaliers to do, marched them up and down the hall among the holly and paper chains to keep them busy.

'It seems to me,' said Professor Branestawm, when Mrs Flittersnoop was telling him what a job it was to get the decorations up, down at the Church Hall, which she did very competently while taking off her hat, tidying her hair and laying the tea, 'it seems to me that all this decorating business makes a great deal of, um, ah, work.'

'Yes, indeed, sir,' said Mrs Flittersnoop. 'And the pity of it is, after all that hanging up of decorations, the lot has to come down again by Twelfth Night.'

'And then,' put in the Professor, 'I suppose it all has to be put up again the next Christmas, and taken down again next, er, Twelfth Night.'

'Well, there it is, sir,' said Mrs Flittersnoop. 'Christmas comes but once a year and when it comes it brings good cheer, as I think somebody said.' She put a plate of mince pies on the table and stuck a sprig of holly in the teapot spout just to make things look festive.

Professor Branestawm had a cup of tea and a mince pie, on which he absent-mindedly spread strawberry jam as he had begun thinking.

'Now wouldn't it be better,' he said, 'if some sort of arrangement could be made whereby the Christmas decorations could be left up until the following Christmas?'

'Oh, but you couldn't do that, sir!' said Mrs Flittersnoop, pouring him out a second cup of tea and just managing to stop him from putting a mince pie in it instead of sugar. 'I mean to say, sir, it wouldn't be right. Leaving the decorations up after Twelfth Night is most unlucky, and it wouldn't seem like Christmas if you had the decorations up all the year.'

The Professor thought it would probably seem like Christmas all the year round, but he didn't say so. He was thinking again.

'No,' he said, pushing bread and butter and mince pies aside and starting to draw on a paper serviette that Mrs Flittersnoop had hurriedly slid under his hand so as to save the tablecloth. 'What is wanted is some means of concealing the Christmas decorations, and bringing them into sight when they are required.'

He gazed out of the window for inspiration and got it immediately. His next door neighbour, on the opposite side to Commander Hardaport, was turning a picture back to front on the wall of his sitting room, and the picture had a white screen on the back for showing holiday slides to unwilling friends. The neighbour hadn't yet drawn his curtains so the Professor could see it all quite clearly in the lighted room.

'The very thing!' he cried. 'Look at that, Mrs Flittersnoop! That's the way to solve the Christmas decorations problem!'

Mrs Flittersnoop didn't see how turning pictures

round to show holiday slides to your friends made putting up Christmas decorations any easier, but she didn't say anything. She had the tea to clear away and some ironing to do and a chapter to finish, and she didn't want to get entangled in one of the Professor's explanations, which were even more difficult to escape from than the Christmas decorations.

Professor Branestawm was in his inventory, with a model of his new invention and with Colonel Dedshott, who kept running round the invention, trying to see what the Professor was showing him and trying to understand what the Professor was telling him, both of which were extremely difficult. In fact, the Colonel's head was going round faster than the Colonel himself.

'No more tiresome work hanging up paper chains and things for Christmas and then taking them down again afterwards,' said the Professor. 'You see this model of a ceiling,' he pointed to something that looked like a small Venetian blind upside down. 'Well, it is made in strips and each strip revolves on its own axis. You follow me?'

'Ha!' grunted the Colonel, who was quite out of breath through trying to follow the Professor round the inventory.

'It is an idea I got from a neighbour who has a cinema screen on the back of a picture,' went on the Professor. 'He turns the picture over when he wants to show films.'

'Ha,' grunted the Colonel again.

'Now,' said the Professor, 'this ceiling looks just like an ordinary ceiling most of the year.'

The Colonel said nothing. He thought it looked like a most extraordinary ceiling.

'But,' said the Professor, getting excited and showering spectacles all over the place, 'if I pull this lever, the sections of ceiling revolve and the Christmas decorations which are fixed to the other side, automatically drop down into position.'

He pulled a lever, the ceiling turned inside out, and paper chains, made of newspaper because the Professor didn't have any coloured paper, dropped gracefully down.

'Jolly good!' grunted the Colonel.

'Then,' went on the Professor, picking up handfuls of spectacles and sawdust from the floor, 'when the time comes to take the decorations down, you do not have to. All you do is to push the lever back.'

He pushed the lever, there was a humming noise, and the paper chains were neatly wound up against the ceiling, which then turned itself inside out again and the decorations vanished.

'My word, Branestawm, what!' cried the Colonel, giving the Professor a slap on the back, which missed as the Professor had moved away, and landed on a sticky gluepot.

'Ah, yes, Dedshott, I rather thought you would say that,' said the Professor, unsticking the gluepot from the Colonel, and giving him a rag covered in blue paint to wipe his hands on. 'People will now be able to enjoy

Christmas decorations without all the bother of putting them up and taking them down.'

'It's a wonderful idea, my dear Professor!' said the Vicar when the Professor explained his new invention.

'And we shall be delighted to have it installed in the Church Hall when we have finished putting up the decorations.'

'Pah!' snorted the Professor, dancing about. 'You don't understand, Vicar. My invention makes it unnecessary for decorations to be put up. You just put up my invention and then it does it all, Christmas after Christmas.'

'Well, I don't know,' said the Vicar, scratching his chin. 'I hardly like to disappoint all the people who are so kindly helping to put up the decorations.'

'Well, you needn't disappoint them, Vicar,' said the Professor. 'They can help to put up my invention instead of the decorations.'

So that was that, and, in due course, the Professor's special revolving ceiling with concealed decorations was installed in the Church Hall.

'Now,' said the Professor, when all the helpers had had cups of tea to revive them after the hard work, 'we shall see how it works.'

He pulled the lever. The ceiling neatly turned itself inside out and down came lovely paper chains and garlands and paper bells. Down also came two gentlemen with long hair and beards and blue overalls. They came down on long strings of tinsel, and swung to and fro.

'Oh, I forgot about Bert and Henry,' said the Professor. They were two professional working gentlemen he had brought along to do some of the awkward parts of the job that required climbing up to the roof and fixing screws with two hands while hanging on with both feet. They had got left behind up in the ceiling by mistake.

'We'll just test it again,' said the Professor.

He touched the lever. There was a humming and whizzing noise. The decorations wound themselves up, Bert and Henry both jumped away just in time, the ceiling turned back on itself and everything was as it had been.

'Hurray!' cried everyone.

'We shall think of you with gratitude, Professor,' beamed the Vicar, over his second cup of tea, 'every year when we do not have to put up the decorations.'

Christmas in Great Pagwell came and went with plenty of presents and Christmas cards and no snow. Twelfth Night came and the Church Hall decorations vanished most efficiently into the ceiling as the Vicar ceremoniously pulled the lever amid cheers from Twelfth Night celebrators.

'Well, that's one invention of mine that hasn't given any trouble,' said the Professor.

'Yes, indeed, I'm sure, sir,' said Mrs Flittersnoop.

Several months later the Pagwell Council were meeting in the Church Hall because the computer had let the Town Hall for a dance on the day the Council meeting was due.

Various matters connected with drains and re-routing the traffic were rapidly dealt with. Then somebody said, 'Isn't this where Professor Branestawm fitted up his mechanical ceiling with Christmas decorations?'

'Why yes, so it is,' said the Mayor.

'Hum, yes, a very clever invention, I've no doubt,' said one of the Councillors, 'but why only the Church Hall? After all the Vicar has plenty of helpers to put up his decorations. He really doesn't need the Professor's double ceiling. I think the idea should be made available to ordinary people, to save them having to put up their decorations without the help which they can't get.'

'This, I fear, is not practical,' said the Mayor. 'The Professor's reversing ceiling would cost too much to put into every house in Pagwell.'

'Why can't the town pay for it?' said a Councillor, who had a shop that sold Christmas decorations.

'That would put the rates up as well as the decorations,' said the Town Clerk.

'Perhaps we could get a government grant,' said the Councillor with the decorations shop.

'Government grants are only for necessities, not for fancywork,' growled the Town Clerk, who had been refused a government grant for changing his bath taps for gold ones.

'Let's start a fund for it then,' suggested the Councillor. At this the Town Clerk became very annoyed and said did he suggest a flag day for revolving ceilings and what did he think the public would say to that.

That started a rowdy argument in which all the Councillors joined.

'Here! Here! Stop all this!' cried the Mayor. 'What on earth are you kicking up all this dust about?'

And whether the Professor's invention thought it ought to answer this question, or whether the rumpus had shaken the machinery, or whether somebody had accidentally knocked against the lever, no one knows. But the entire ceiling turned itself inside out and down came not only the Christmas decorations but also a great deal of very dusty dust. Everyone became covered with it.

'Help! Pwoof! Splutter!' gasped the Mayor. The Town Clerk grabbed the lever and pushed it.

'Be careful of those paper chains!' cried the Councillor, who had the shop that sold Christmas decorations and who didn't like too see them being ill-treated. He snatched at the lever and pulled it back, but before the ceiling was half revolved two more Councillors, determined to be helpful, were wagging the lever to and fro. *Click, clank, plop*, the reversible ceiling did its best to turn inside out and outside in both at once.

Then the Town Clerk saw one of those poles for opening and shutting high windows, that was lying on the floor of the hall. With a yell he picked it up and pushed it into the rapidly revolving ceiling.

'That'll stop it!' he cried.

It didn't.

A Branestawm invention wasn't going to stand for being poked with a window pole. Motors began to whir,

paper chains and garlands began to swing to and fro.
They got entangled in the Mayor's chain, pulled it off
and swung it away with them. The Mayor had to duck
behind the table to avoid being hit with his own chain.

The ceiling turned inside out again to let out a lot
more dust it had found. Everywhere was like a foggy
day. Councillors choked and coughed and spluttered.
The Town Clerk climbed out of the window, and ran
straight into the Vicar.

'Dear, dear, dear!' said the Vicar, when he saw what
was happening. 'I fear this is very irregular.'

Just then Professor Branestawm arrived.

'Good gracious!' he exclaimed. 'I, er, trust you have
not, ah, damaged my invention, gentlemen?' He went
to the lever and pulled it. Nothing happened, as everything that could happen had already done so. He pushed the lever. He worked it up and down. A bunch of
paper chains enveloped him and swung him up to the
ceiling, which opened, let him half way through and
closed again.

'It's got the Professor!' wailed the Mayor. 'Help!'

Crash! Plop! Bang! The Professor kicked and strug-
gled, but the ceiling held him fast.

The Mayor dashed out of the Hall and ran into Mrs
Flittersnoop, who was on her way to her sister Aggie's
for a quiet look at the telly, and a spot of crochet.

'The Professor!' gasped the Mayor. 'He's being eaten
by his own ceiling! Help!'

Mrs Flittersnoop rushed into the Hall. 'Oh dear, a
dearie me, I'm sure!' she cried. Two gilt angels came

at her but she beat them off with her umbrella. More dust and decorations showered down.

Mrs Flittersnoop threw her crochet into the works. That did it. The ceiling let go of the Professor who dropped with a crash on to the table. Gilt angels, paper bells, garlands and chains collapsed everywhere.

'I think perhaps,' said the Professor, when Mrs Flittersnoop had got him home safely and telephoned sister Aggie to postpone the crochet and telly until another evening, 'I think perhaps it is just as well we did not get my Christmas decorations invention installed in any private houses. You were right, Mrs Flittersnoop, and it does seem to be unlucky to leave Christmas decorations up after Twelfth Night. However well you hide them.'

'Yes, indeed, I'm sure, sir,' said Mrs Flittersnoop.

7

The Awful Omelette Story

'I SIMPLY cannot stand omelettes,' said Mrs Flittersnoop to her sister Aggie, as they were having a nice cup of coffee together.

'But I always thought you were partial to a nice omelette,' said sister Aggie, who was partial to a great many things herself.

'Well, yes, I was,' said Mrs Flittersnoop. 'Omelettes are very good in their way, but you can have too much of a good thing, as I always say, and, after five weeks of omelettes, and nothing but omelettes, well, I mean to say . . .'

It all happened, of course, as a result of one of Professor Branestawm's inventions.

Mrs Flittersnoop was going to buy one of those frying pans that don't let things stick to them while cooking, and she happened to mention this to the Professor at breakfast.

Before she could get the breakfast cleared away and the place tidied up and the waste paper put out for the dustmen, and her shopping things on and her shopping list made out on the back of a page of last year's calendar from Ginnibag & Knitwoddle's, the Professor had worked out a devastatingly domestic invention for a non-stick omelette pan with fringe benefits.

It was a very simple contrivance, as Branestawm contrivances went. It had no visible machinery, wires did not hang from it anywhere, there was a complete absence of buttons for pushing and a lack of levers for pulling. In fact, it looked like an ordinary omelette pan except that it was pale green, stood on legs, had an electronically-controlled timing device, an egg-timer, an anti-splutter guard, a self-ejecting omelette remover and built-in protection against over-cooking. It also washed itself, dried itself up and, if you showed it the cupboard, it put itself away.

'Very clever, I'm sure, sir,' said Mrs Flittersnoop, eyeing it rather warily.

'There's only one thing,' said the Professor, wagging his finger. 'This is a specifically specialized, er, device. It is designed to make omelettes and nothing else. It cannot be used for, um, ah, boiling ham or, ah, making cakes or dusting the furniture, you understand.'

'Well, as I always say,' said Mrs Flittersnoop to sister Aggie over a nice cup of tea, 'one thing at a time and that done well is better than trying to do everything and not getting anything done.'

'But I'm surprised you're ready to risk it,' said sister Aggie. 'I mean, the things you've had to put up with from the Professor's inventions. Not but what he doesn't mean well, the poor gentleman, but those machines of his are apt to go on and on so. Have another cup of tea.'

'Yes, I know, Aggie,' said Mrs Flittersnoop, not minding if she did. 'But try anything once, as I always say. After all, a little thing like an omelette pan can't do any harm and if it doesn't work omelettes I can always fall back on my copper-bottomed frying pan.'

'Well, you must speak as you find,' said sister Aggie, who didn't fancy falling back on copper-bottomed frying pans herself. 'And there's always the spare room ready for you if this new thing of the Professor's gets troublesome.'

So Mrs Flittersnoop, undaunted by past affrays with Branestawm inventions, determined to give the Professor's ingenious omelette pan a fair trial, crossed her fingers, threw some salt over her left shoulder, put on her cooking apron and began on a ham omelette for the Professor's lunch.

She put the eggs into the pan which cooked them into a nice flat omelette, and blew a polite whistle when the centre part was just right. She added chopped ham, the pan folded the omelette over itself and delivered the finished article neatly on to a plate it had previously heated.

'Well, I never!' said Mrs Flittersnoop. And she served the omelette to the Professor, who ate it all up without once dropping his spectacles in it or putting it in his pocket or absent-mindedly trying to write notes on it, which showed what a remarkable omelette it was.

'I will say it's a great help,' said Mrs Flittersnoop to

sister Aggie later on, over a nice glass of orangeade. 'I mean, omelettes are tricky things, as you well know, Aggie, but this time I'd no cause to worry. I didn't even lock the kitchen door while I was cooking it, to avoid interruptions, omelettes being things you have to concentrate on. But this pan of the Professor's does all its own concentrating and no washing up either.'

'Well, I hope you're right,' said sister Aggie. 'But one never knows with the Professor's inventions, and we must hope for the best.'

The wonderful omelette pan was such a success that the Professor felt he ought to show it off to his friends.

'You mean, you want to ask people to an omelette lunch sir?' said Mrs Flittersnoop, who didn't mind the idea at all, with the Professor's invention to do it all for her.

The lunch began with a large mushroom omelette for everyone, followed by a small jam omelette by way of a sweet and finished off with little tiny cheese omelettes as savouries.

'Best omelettes I've ever tasted!' said Commander Hardaport, who had been used to ships' omelettes made at sea in rough weather by sailor cooks.

'My word, yes, by Jove!' cried Colonel Dedshott, whose Catapult Cavalier butlers never tried to make omelettes as they thought they were too French and anyway found the ordinary military fried eggs easier.

Dr Mumpzanmeazle declared that if people ate more omelettes they would be less likely to be under-nourished, but added a warning that if people ate too many omelettes they might become well over-nourished.

The Mayor ate his omelette without having to declare it open first. Miss Frenzie of the Pagwell Publishing Company was inspired with the idea of getting out a recipe book on *Ten thousand omelettes you can make at home*. And the Professor was so occupied trying to explain what an ingenious device his omelette pan was, that he rolled his omelette up and pushed it into his serviette ring where it made a squishy mess on the tablecloth.

'Well, I think that we may congratulate ourselves, Mrs Flittersnoop,' he said, when the guests had gone off full of praise and good omelettes. 'This latest idea of mine seems to leave nothing to be desired.'

And although Mrs Flittersnoop felt that it had left something not to be desired in the squishy mess the Professor had made on the tablecloth, she didn't complain.

Next day Mrs Flittersnoop thought the Professor had had enough of omelettes for the time being, so she decided to cook him a nice kipper for his breakfast. And she used the omelette pan because it cleaned itself and saved the washing up.

Sizzle, suzzle, pop, pop, flip, went the pan, blew its whistle and ejected on to a pre-warmed plate a kipper that was well mashed-up and neatly folded into a flat omelette shape.

'Good gracious!' said Mrs Flittersnoop.

But it might well have been roast beef, strawberry

jam and haricot beans for all the Professor noticed because he was deep in a new invention for a computer to check mistakes made by computers, and he was having difficulty over the bit that stopped the mistake-detecting computer from making mistakes itself and detecting mistakes which the other computers hadn't made.

That evening Mrs Flittersnoop tried to do herself a fried fillet sole, but the omelette pan turned it into a sole omelette.

She decided she would fall back on her copper-bottomed frying pan, but then she discovered that the Professor had borrowed it for inventing purposes, and it was full of self-stick paint and assorted screws. She couldn't even fall back on any of her ordinary non-copper-bottomed pans, because the Professor had borrowed them as well, thinking she would not need them now she had his marvellous non-stick omelette pan. And so she was forced to try to make the Professor's supper in that.

The omelette pan turned fried potatoes into potato omelettes, it made bubble and squeak into bubble and squeak omelettes, and in fact it omelettized everything that was put into it.

'Oh dear, oh dear, good gracious me!' exclaimed Mrs Flittersnoop. 'Aggie was right. I should never have touched it.'

But it was too late. The omelette pan began to affect all the equipment in the kitchen. A golden syrup pudding came out of the oven as a golden syrup omelette.

Mrs Flittersnoop's celebrated fruit cake became Genoa omelette. She got lemon cheese tart omelettes and grilled lamb cutlet omelettes with small mint sauce omelettes whether she liked it or not.

'Oh, whatever shall I do?' groaned Mrs Flittersnoop, struggling hard to stop a Swiss roll turning into a Swiss roll omelette but not succeeding. And when it came to dry toast omelettes and rice crispie omelettes, it was more than Mrs Flittersnoop and human nature could stand. So she went to sister Aggie where, thank goodness, there was always the spare bedroom free from omelettes.

Professor Branestawm soon grew tired of finding that whenever he did remember to eat anything it was some kind of crazy omelette and started having his meals out.

Commander Hardaport offered to drop depth charges on the omelettes as they appeared but that would only have made a mess on the linoleum.

Then the omelette pan, aided and abetted by the rest of the kitchen, started making omelettes of everything in sight. Knife and fork omelettes, china plate omelettes and instant coffee omelettes came pouring out. Teacloth omelettes wrapped themselves round biological detergent omelettes. Furniture polish omelettes and tin opener omelettes were everywhere.

'Oh dear, why ever did I invent an omelette pan?' groaned the Professor, as omelettes clashed and rattled round him. He pushed the machine into a cupboard and locked the door, but the omelette pan picked the lock with a fork and shot out again with three omelettes made out of the wine glasses that had been in the cupboard.

'Help!' cried the Professor. He dashed out into the street, narrowly avoiding a spotted omelette made from Mrs Flittersnoop's apron that the omelette pan threw at him out of the kitchen window. 'Help! Call Colonel Dedshott! Omelette pan out of control! Help!'

Fortunately Dr Mumpzanmeazle was going past in his car, and gave him a lift to Colonel Dedshott's house. They arrived just as the Colonel was deciding not to have an omelette for lunch.

In no time at all the Colonel and his Catapult Cavaliers shot back to the Professor's house, and subdued the

militant omelette pan assisted by encouraging remarks
through a loud hailer from Commander Hardaport
who had steamed over to help. They all got the kitchen
a bit tidied up so that the Professor could send a telegam
to Mrs Flittersnoop saying, 'Return at once, all is well.'

'Well, I can't bring myself to look an omelette in the
face any more, Aggie,' she said to her sister a few days
later over a nice cup of cocoa.

Neither could the Professor, if it came to that, and
he gave the marvellous omelette pan to Ye Olde Bun
Shoppe, which opened a special inner shop which they
called Ye Olde Omelette Place. And there the omelette
pan could happily go on turning out omelettes of every
kind without let or hindrance.

But neither the Professor nor Mrs Flittersnoop ever
went near it. They had had enough omelettes.

8

Professor Branestawm Goes Cuckoo

MECHANICAL popping noises took place outside Professor Branestawm's house, and two small clouds of smoke drifted past his window. But it wasn't an invention of the Professor's. It was someone arriving.

Mrs Flittersnoop opened the door in her usual genteel manner and said, 'Thank you very much, I'm sure.' Then the noises burst out again, the clouds of smoke reversed past the window and the noises faded rapidly in the distance.

'From the Vicar, sir,' said Mrs Flittersnoop, coming into the Professor's study with a small but very knobbly parcel.

'Dear me!' said the Professor, looking at the parcel under and over various pairs of spectacles. 'I had no idea the Vicar went about in such an, er, excitable manner.'

'No, sir,' said Mrs Flittersnoop. 'It wasn't the Vicar who brought it, sir, it was his daughters, Maisie and Daisie. In their cars, sir,' she added, and then said, 'Good gracious me, indeed, sir!' as the Professor got the parcel undone.

An ornamental and very Black Forest-looking clock

fell out on the table. A determined little bird shot out of a trapdoor, said 'Cuckoo!' three times and shot back again.

'A cuckoo clock!' cried Mrs Flittersnoop. 'How nice of the Vicar!'

'Tut! tut!' said the Professor. 'It is not at all nice of the Vicar. I really do not understand it. That is to say, why doesn't he like it?'

'Like what, sir?' asked Mrs Flittersnoop.

'I sent this clock to the Vicar,' said the Professor, 'knowing that he favours traditional kinds of, ah, things, but apparently he has taken offence. He has sent it back without a word.'

The Vicar had done nothing of the kind. He had never seen the clock. Professor Branestawm had bought it at a little shop to send to the Vicar. But he had written his own address on the label instead of the Vicar's. Then Maisie and Daisie, the Vicar's twin daughters, happened to call at the shop later in their twin motor cars, and the shopman asked them to deliver it to the Professor's, as his delivery van had broken down.

Just then the telephone rang.

'I hope you got the parcel safely,' said the Vicar's voice. 'My girls said they had taken it over.'

Then there was a lot of mixed-up explaining, by the end of which the Vicar had made it clear that there was nothing in this world he would like so much as a cuckoo clock, except perhaps a new organ for the church or a new church for the organ. And Professor Branestawm was under the impression that the Vicar didn't like the cuckoo clock under discussion but rather fancied having one invented by the Professor.

'Hm!' said the Professor, 'I suppose he wants a cuckoo clock that sings hymns at the quarter hours, or reminds him when to say his sermon . . . Ha!' The Professor clapped a hand to his head and sent spectacles flying into the air. 'What an idea! A cuckoo clock that instead of just saying "Cuckoo" when the hour strikes, gives helpful reminders. It's never been done before. I shall be the first person in the world to invent a genuine automatic reminding non-cuckoo clock. My name will go down to er, er . . .'

The next minute he was off to his inventory. Mrs Flittersnoop hung the cuckoo clock carefully on the wall and wound it up.

More mechanical noises were taking place, not outside the Professor's house this time but inside his inventory.

Bong! Bong! Bong! Bong! rang out cracked chimes, and then an even more cracked voice said, 'Remember to choose the hymns for evening service.'

'Ha!' said the Professor gazing with some admiration at his newly invented non-cuckoo clock. It looked like a cross between a small cathedral and a cinema. It had a throng of angels round the bottom and a tower at the top. From this tower, through a gothic door, emerged a little bird in a cassock whenever the chimes rang out.

'Excellent!' murmured the Professor. He moved the hands of the clock round another hour. The chimes sounded again, and the cassocked cuckoo shot out and said, 'Pray remember to put your surplice out for the laundry,' and shot in again.

'Very satisfying!' said the Professor. 'Now I must find out exactly what things a Vicar wants to be reminded about, and then I can finish the clock and present it.'

But finding out what a Vicar might want to be reminded of was rather difficult. Mrs Flittersnoop was all for having the clock remind him to change his underwear and not be late for dinner. The Dean of Great Pagwell considered the reminders should be concerned with church matters such as matins and evensong and harvest festival. The verger wanted the reminder clock put over the pulpit to tell the congregation please to replace the prayer books before leaving, to save him having to do it. Dr Mumpzanmeazle thought it presented an excellent opportunity for warning people of the dangers of infection in crowded buildings. Colonel Dedshott thought the cuckoo shouldn't remind but should command, and Commander Hardaport (Retired) thought it should give gale warnings and shipping forecasts, although why the Vicar should need these wasn't clear.

All this expert advice didn't help the Professor much with the Vicar's clock. But it gave him a new idea and made him decide to make reminder clocks for all his friends.

'They're very fond of saying I am, er, absent-minded,' he said, taking a sip of ink in mistake for his morning coffee, and wondering why it tasted cold. 'I shall show them that my mind is sufficiently present to remind them, as it were, by remote control, of the things they should have remembered but may not have.'

For some time the Professor worked hard on inventing non-cuckoo reminding clocks for his friends. Then he invited them all to one of his celebrated demonstrations, while Mrs Flittersnoop, reinforced by her sister Aggie and a few friends, prepared suitable refreshments.

By the time Colonel Dedshott, the Vicar, the Mayor, Commander Hardaport (Retired), and everybody else the Professor had invited were pressed into the Professor's dining room, along with the clocks, which took up nearly as much space as they did, nobody had any room to eat and only just enough room to speak.

'This one is for the Mayor,' said the · Professor, starting up a municipal-looking clock with the arms of Great Pagwell on the front and *No parking* notices on each side.

Ding! Dong! 'Remember to declare open M592 motorway between Great Pagwell and Pagwell Green,' croaked a little bird in a cocked hat.

'Hrrrrm!' said the Mayor.

'And here is one for Commander Hardaport,' said the Professor, getting under way a clock with several funnels, and two masts. It had weights shaped like anchors.

Dong-dong! Dong-dong! Dong-dong! Dong-dong! The clock very properly rang up eight bells, and a small seagull in a naval cap with a telescope under its wing shouted very crisply, 'Belay there, weed the starboard flower bed!'

'Aye, aye!' cried the Commander.

'Now for the Doctor's clock,' continued the Professor.

A medical clock, with red crosses on its sides and a strong smell of antiseptic, went, *Ding-ding-ding-ding!* like a frantic ambulance. Then out shot a little bird in nurse's uniform and snapped, 'Time for a spot check on patients in surgery, please, Doctor!' It brandished a thermometer and shot in again.

Colonel Dedshotts' clock resembled a military tent, emitted a bugle call instead of a chime, and a little sergeant bird clicked himself to attention and roared out, 'By the left, change socks!' clicked again and vanished.

'My word, by Jove, what!' exclaimed the Colonel.

Other non-cuckoo reminding clocks for the Vicar, Lord Pagwell of the Pagwell Publishing Company, the Headmaster of Pagwell College and other dignified friends of the Professor all performed suitably. Then Mrs Flittersnoop popped out of the kitchen like a rather large cuckoo herself and announced refreshments, which had to be taken in the front garden as there was no eating room anywhere else.

'Remarkable invention of the Professor's, I must say,' said the Mayor.

When everyone had had as much to eat as they wanted, or as much as they could get before someone else got it, the party broke up. The Professor's friends went home carrying their special clocks. Mrs Flitter-snoop and her friends tackled the washing up and the spare refreshments they had had the foresight to hide away for later use. And the Professor went happily off to give a lecture he wasn't due to give until next Tuesday.

But the next morning Colonel Dedshott had his breakfast interrupted by the sergeant bird from his clock, who shot out, sprang to attention, and bellowed, 'Fall in to choose hymns for evening service!'

The same afternoon Dr Mumpzanmeazle's clock rang its ambulance bell, and the nurse bird cried, 'Foundation stone for the new primary school to be laid three times a day after meals!'

The Doctor rushed out of the house and collided with Commander Hardaport who was steaming past his gate.

'Ha, Doctor!' cried the Commander. 'Funny thing happened this morning. That confounded clock Professor Branestawm made for me started reminding me to give anti-flu injections to the lifeboats. Said my port engine was suffering from rheumatism. How'd it get mixed up with your clock, hey?'

The Doctor was on the point of telling him about his clock when the Vicar came wobbling past on his bicycle, carrying his reminder clock which was singing out, 'Don't forget to scrub the decks; swab the scuppers out!' to the tune of *Onward Christian Soldiers*. Also coming down the road were the Mayor, Lord Pagwell and the Chief of the Fire Brigade, each clutching a clock.

'We must return these contraptions to the Professor at once!' the Mayor was saying. 'I am afraid they may utter some instructions that will be contrary to the bye-laws.'

Dr Mumpzanmeazle dashed into his house and came out with his clock.

'To the Professor's!' he cried. 'Most urgent! We don't want to let this develop into an epidemic.'

They all shot off, collected Colonel Dedshott and the Vicar, and surged round to Professor Branestawm's house with all the clocks telling them what to do and when to do it.

'Ah, yes,' said the Professor, when he had managed to get the clocks to stop shouting and Colonel Dedshott and the rest to stop talking. 'I rather fear it was a mistake to bring the clocks together for my demonstration. The juxtaposition of their electronic mechanisms has possibly caused some unwise integration of the radio active waves between them.'

'Sounds like mutiny to me!' cried Commander Hardaport. 'Clap 'em in irons, I say!'

'Vast heaving!' cried the Commander's clock.

'Stop talking in the ranks there!' shouted the Colonel clock.

'Change your vest three times a day before giving a sermon on bad drains,' retorted the Doctor's clock.

'Who are you calling a drain?' bellowed Lord Pagwell's clock to the Doctor's.

'Shut up!' retorted the Doctor's clock.

Then a great argument broke out among the clocks.
They called one another rude names. They commanded
one another to get knotted, drop dead, and jump in
lakes.

'As you were!' shouted Colonel Dedshott, sounding
like his own sergeant bird but much louder. He hit the
clock with a poker. It collapsed and the bird sergeant
squawked, 'Turn out the guard! Who goes there with
foundation stones and hymn books?'

Then the other clocks started throwing their weights
about. The Commander's clock hooked the Mayor's
clock with one of its anchor-shaped weights and pulled
two *No parking* notices off it. The Mayor's clock re-
taliated with a direct hit on the Vicar's angels. The
Commander's clock joined forces with the Doctor's
clock and wound their chains round the Colonel's clock
which was reading out the ten commandments.

Colonel Dedshott and Commander Hardaport grabbed a handful of fire irons.

'Take them in the rear, Commander!' bellowed
Colonel Dedshott. 'I'll attack from the flank.'

Commander Hardaport leapt out of the window,
and was instantly arrested by two policemen looking
for promotion.

'Now then,' they said, 'what's all this?'

The answer came as the clocks threw the Colonel out
of the French doors.

Chaos and confusion reigned. Colonel Dedshott
snatched a policeman's walkie-talkie and tried to call
up the Catapult Cavaliers. But, before the police station

he contacted could sort things out, the pandemonium in the Professor's house began to die down of its own accord, as the clocks finally demolished one another. Then with the help of the Fifth Upper Pagwell Troop of Scouts, who happened to be passing by, the Professor's house was tidied up and the bits of demolished clocks safely stowed in the most distant municipal rubbish dump.

Mrs Flittersnoop was just handing round cups of tea, which everyone felt much in need of, when there was a click, and a little voice said, 'Cuckoo!' several times.

'Oh, my goodness me!' cried Mrs Flittersnoop. 'Don't say those clocks have come back!'

'Er, no, it's quite all right,' said the Professor, stirring an empty cup before Mrs Flittersnoop was sufficiently calmed down to pour tea into it. 'That will be the original cuckoo clock I bought for the Vicar. It has, I fear, been overlooked.'

'You bought it for *me*?' said the Vicar. 'Surely that is the clock my daughters delivered from the shop to *you*?'

So the misunderstanding was sorted out, and the Professor gave the cuckoo clock to the Vicar, who was very pleased to have a nice ordinary cuckoo clock with no bright ideas and no desire to give imitations of anybody.

9

Knit Two Together

'Um,' said Professor Branestawm. 'They look very nice but . . .'

'You don't want to buy one of those,' said Mrs Flittersnoop. 'I can make one for you.'

She had accompanied the Professor to Ginnibag & Knitwoddle's to help him buy a nice, warm, woolly waistcoat, and to make sure he got to Ginnibag & Knitwoddle's without being sidetracked into the ironmongers and coming home with a bag of mixed nails instead of a woolly waistcoat.

But when she saw the prices, Mrs Flittersnoop waved her hands in horror.

'They are certainly rather expensive,' murmered the Professor, looking at a purple waistcoat and seeing 42 printed on it, which he thought meant pounds but really meant inches.

'I can knit you one much better than any of these, I'm sure, sir,' said Mrs Flittersnoop, rummaging disdainfully through piles of woolly waistcoats. 'It will be a good opportunity for me to try out the new way of knitting you invented for me.' The Professor had worked out a special method that was a cross between knitting and crochet, but was twice as fast as either, and could be done with one hand while the other hand did the ironing or made the tea.

'But you are going away for your holidays,' said the Professor. 'I, er, don't think you ought to spend your holidays knitting me woolly waistcoats.'

'But why ever not, sir?' exclaimed Mrs Flittersnoop, who now had a definite woolly waistcoat gleam in her eye.

Just then the Professor's attention was attracted by another counter where a girl in a tall hair style was demonstrating a machine that knitted things, and he wandered away to watch.

'Yes,' said Mrs Flittersnoop to herself, 'I'll knit a nice woolly waistcoat for the Professor while I'm away on holiday. It will be something to keep me occupied. I never was one for idling away my time, and what with all that sea and sand stretching away to goodness knows where, there isn't all that much to look at and you enjoy a holiday all the more if you keep yourself occupied, I always say. It'll be a suprise for the Professor when I get back.'

The Professor was also thinking about woolly waistcoats, but with mechanical connections. And by the time he reached home he had a new invention rolling round inside his head.

'Well, I'm just off, sir,' said Mrs Flittersnoop, a few days later. 'Here's a list of the things you mustn't forget to do,' she said, giving the Professor a sheet of paper crammed with tiny writing on both sides. 'And here's my address just in case.' She didn't say in case of what. 'And I hope you'll have a nice time with the Colonel, sir.'

'Um, ah, thank you,' said the Professor, taking the pieces of paper and putting them behind the clock, which wasn't much good because he was going to stay with Colonel Dedshott. But Mrs Flittersnoop had carefully given the Colonel a copy of the 'things you mustn't forget' list, which the Colonel had pinned with military precision on a little green baize notice board in the Professor's room. This also had pinned to it various notices saying when to parade for breakfast and what time 'lights out' was and other matters calculated to make the household run smoothly.

So everything seemed nicely organized for Mrs Flittersnoop to go away with an easy mind, and with her sister Aggie and sister Aggie's little Esme, as well as three suitcases, a string bag, a packet of sandwiches for the journey, several magazines to read on the way, a sunshade in case of sun, an umbrella in case of rain, and little Esme's bucket and spade and fishing net for fine weather and drawing and painting books for indoor weather.

'I thought I'd knit the Professor a nice woolly waistcoat while we're away,' said Mrs Flittersnoop to sister Aggie, as they sat in the train. 'It will be a nice surprise for him, and a good opportunity to try out my new way of knitting.'

'Well, I do think that's thoughtful of you,' said sister

Aggie. 'And I tell you what I'll do. I'll knit a woolly waistcoat for the Vicar, just to keep you company.'

So, as soon as they had got themselves settled in at the quiet little hotel at the seaside (which wasn't very soon actually because the hotel was run by a distant cousin of sister Aggie's, who had a lot to talk about, and Mrs Flittersnoop thought she should do her share of talking too) they went out to buy wool.

'I thought a quiet grey,' said Mrs Flittersnoop, in the seaside wool shop.

'Well, I was thinking more of a cheerful mauve,' said sister Aggie.

'Can I have a raspberry milk-shake?' asked Esme.

'Don't you think crushed strawberry would be better?' said Mrs Flittersnoop, meaning the wool.

'Tastes the same as raspberry,' said Esme, who was an experienced milk-shake consumer.

'Well, I don't know,' said sister Aggie. 'As it's for the Vicar we'd better be careful about the colour. I mean to say, we don't want to give him a woolly waistcoat of the wrong colour for wearing at Advent, or too bright for Lent . . .'

'I think you're quite right, I'm sure,' said Mrs Flittersnoop. 'A nice quiet grey, as I said, would be safest, and I'll use the same for the Professor. And then if we buy both lots of wool together we can make them give us a discount for quantity.'

'Right,' said sister Aggie. They bought the wool. They insisted on their discount, they picked up their parcels, and then all three went up to the Balcony

Restaurant overlooking the sea, and the two ladies had coffee and cream cakes and never mind the calories, while Esme had a raspberry milk-shake and a bag of onion-flavoured barbecue crisps.

Back in Great Pagwell Professor Branestawm was showing Colonel Dedshott his new invention, which he had constructed in the stable where the Colonel kept his horse, while the horse had moved out into the shed where the Colonel's Catapult Cavalier butlers kept the garden tools, which had been moved out into a kennel where the people who used to live there had kept a dog.

'The ordinary knitting machine,' said the Professor, waving spectacles about, 'has to be operated by hand. There is a great deal of, er, pushing things to and fro. My invention makes all that unnecessary.'

'Ha, my word!' grunted the Colonel, not knowing what else to grunt.

The Professor pointed to some dials and switches. 'These are the selectors for the type of garment required,' he explained. 'And one can choose the pattern and colour to be used.'

'Yes, rather!' said the Colonel, drinking his tea before the Professor did anything drastic to it.

'I shall now knit a nice woolly waistcoat for myself. It will be a surprise for Mrs Flittersnoop when she gets back from her holiday,' said the Professor, pulling levers and twisting dials.

Zim! Clicketty click! went the machine. It made all

the usual knitting noises, and out shot a pullover with three yellow sleeves and two pink ones.

'Er, ah, um,' said the Professor, peering at it. 'Some adjustment is necessary.'

He switched and dialled again.

Clicketty zim! Zimmetty click! went the machine and a purple cardigan three yards long and two inches wide came snaking out.

The Professor made a few more adjustments, which resulted in a pair of trousers with one short leg and one very long one. After this a waistcoat appeared at last, but it was one yard square, with seven pockets, two zip fasteners, seventeen buttons and a wide turn-down collar.

'Tut, tut!' muttered the Professor. 'This is most troublesome!'

'Here, let me have a go,' said the Colonel. He leant over, twisted a dial and pressed all the switches at once.

The machine shrieked, sent out puffs of coloured smoke, and then produced a khaki pullover with sergeants' stripes on one arm and a sergeant major's crown on the other, a belt decorated with pink daisies and several pockets filled with imitation knitted bullets.

'Oh dear,' said the Professor, 'I'm afraid it looks as if I shall have to buy myself a waistcoat after all.'

Meanwhile Mrs Flittersnoop and sister Aggie were comfortably settled on the beach, sitting in the shade of a motor boat and knitting and nattering at full speed.

'I do hope the Professor will be pleased with his

waistcoat,' said Mrs Flittersnoop, holding up a large piece of knitting. She had nearly finished, but sister Aggie, who was a slower knitter but faster talker, still had one ball of wool to go.

'I'll just pop over to the cafe and get some ginger beer and buns,' said Mrs Flittersnoop, and off she went, while sister Aggie divided her attention between making sure she was doing Mrs Flittersnoop's specially invented kind of knitting in the right way, and seeing what Esme was up to and telling her to stop.

At this moment, a passing dog, who was also spending his holidays by the sea, came across sister Aggie's remaining ball of wool, picked it up carefully in his mouth and went off to do a bit of his own kind of knitting with it. Sister Aggie never noticed.

Mrs Flittersnoop returned and ginger beer drinking and bun eating took over from knitting and nattering.

'I see they're getting the illuminations ready,' said sister Aggie, gazing at the promenade, while she groped for the end, or rather the beginning, of the new ball of wool that wasn't there.

'Yes, indeed, I'm sure,' said Mrs Flittersnoop, tidily burying the empty bun bag so as not to leave litter.

And she didn't notice that sister Aggie had picked up by mistake the end of the wool that Mrs Flittersnoop herself was knitting with. Aggie fastened this to the end of her own knitting and started purling and plaining and passing over slip stitches as fast as she could.

But as fast as she knitted her woolly waistcoat for the Vicar, she unkitted Mrs Flittersnoop's woolly waistcoat for Professor Branestawm. Neither of them realized what was happening. Mrs Flittersnoop wasn't knitting. She was having a rest and enjoying the scenery, which included several shops on the promenade, a fierce warning about not bathing near dangerous rocks, and a distant view of the gas works.

Clicketty, clicketty, click! went sister Aggie, and the Vicar's waistcoat grew slowly at the expense of the Professor's, which became smaller and smaller.

Back at the Colonel's house things were no better. The Professor had just made another attempt to knit

a woolly waistcoat, but his machine had produced a free-standing dressing gown in thick fisherman's wool, and was now starting on a set of reversible egg cosies in cable stitch.

When sister Aggie had knitted exactly the same amount of the Vicar's waistcoat as there was left of the Professor's, she paused to wonder where Esme had got to, and Mrs Flittersnoop, who had had enough of the scenery for the moment, picked up her needles and went on with her own knitting.

And of course, as she knitted the Professor's waistcoat, so she undid the Vicar's because both ladies were knitting with different ends of the same wool.

Then Esme came back with an ice-cream cornet. Sister Aggie began knitting again, and the two waistcoats grew larger and smaller alternately, as the knitting speed of the two absorbed ladies varied.

'Well, I declare!' said Mrs Flittersnoop, as the clock on the pier struck one. 'If it isn't lunch time already! We must be getting back, Aggie, or the shepherd's pie will be cold.'

So they started to pack their knitting into enormous knitting bags, along with all the other things you simply have to have with you on the beach. Then up came a boatman.

'Sorry to disturb you, ladies,' he said. 'But, unless you fancy a motor boat trip round the lighthouse, I'll have to ask you to get up.'

'No, indeed, I'm sure, sir,' said Mrs Flittersnoop, a

bit flustered. And she and Aggie moved out of the way of the boat. The boatman, helped by several friends, pushed the boat into the sea, and went chugging off.

But oh dear! The wool between Aggie's knitting and Mrs Flittersnoop's had got caught round some nautical part of the boat and was being carried out to sea, undoing both the Vicar's woolly waistcoat and the Professor's as it went.

Mrs Flittersnoop and sister Aggie didn't notice what was happening because they were too concerned about the shepherd's pie. Back to the hotel they went, talking away, while their knitting disappeared rapidly out to sea on a motor boat for a trip round the lighthouse.

'How are you getting on with that waistcoat?' the Colonel was asking.

'It's hopeless,' said the Professor. 'The wretched machine seems to have given up trying. It now appears to be knitting a clockwork train.'

'Let's see how we've got on,' said Mrs Flittersnoop, after lunch. She opened her knitting bag and gave a shriek.

'Good gracious, Aggie!' she cried. 'Whatever's happened to my knitting?'

'You must have left it on the beach,' said Aggie. Then she to gave a shriek when she found she hadn't got her knitting either.

'I can't understand it,' cried Mrs Flittersnoop. 'We'd

nearly finished those waistcoats, and now where are they?'

But, if Mrs Flittersnoop and sister Aggie were puzzled about their knitting, the coastguards were even more puzzled by a strange wool slick found floating in the sea. They had never seen a wool slick before and didn't know what to do with it.

When Mrs Flittersnoop returned to Great Pagwell she decided not to say anything to the Professor about the lovely woolly waistcoat she thought she had knitted for him. She felt it would be a disappointment, and besides, she didn't know what the Professor would think of her for knitting a woolly waistcoat and then finding she had lost it.

She brought him back a little box covered with shells, which was just what the Professor wanted for keeping his screws and nails and bits of wire in.

The Professor didn't say anything to Mrs Flittersnoop either about the woolly waistcoat he tried to knit. But he managed to give his knitting machine away to the Ladies' Guild of Good Works, who thought it would be a nice idea to make it knit stair carpet for lighthouses. So, one way and another, all the knitting that the Professor and Mrs Flittersnoop did that summer went out to sea.

10

The Impossible Invention

'WELL, I do think that's kind of the Professor!' exclaimed Mrs Flittersnoop, as she came into the kitchen
and found a neat little pair of steps waiting for her.
'I always did say how nice it would be to have some
steps to reach those top cupboards and now the Professor has invented some for me.'

Professor Branestawm had done nothing of the kind.
Of course, if he *had* remembered that Mrs Flittersnoop
wanted steps to reach the top cupboards, he would
certainly have invented the most outrageous mechanical self-extending, double-folding, collapsible and vari-
ously adjustable pair of steps, no doubt with attach-
ments for opening sardine tins without mashing up the
sardines and for decarbonizing burnt toast.

But he hadn't remembered, and so he didn't invent
anything of the kind. The little pair of steps had been
delivered by the Great Pagwell Furnishing Store, because of a mistake by their new computer. The steps
should have been delivered to Mr Hokkibats who had
some new ingenious idea for a game of outdoor ludo
played while running up and down steps.

Mrs Flittersnoop, of course, didn't know all this. She

went off to look for the Professor and thank him for the steps.

She looked in his inventory and in his study and several other places where the Professor wasn't.

'Oh well, I expect he's gone out,' she said to herself. 'I'll just get the breakfast things cleared away.'

'Good gracious me!' she exclaimed, when she got back to the kitchen. The little pair of steps had turned itself into a table.

'Well, there, now,' she said. 'If that isn't clever of the Professor! When I don't need the steps to get at the top cupboards it turns into a table where I can make out my shopping lists.'

But of course it hadn't. Pagwell Furnishing Store had found out their mistake about the steps, because Mr Hokkibats had been on the telephone for twenty minutes, telling them what sort of furnishing store they were. So they had taken away the steps and replaced them with a table which ought to have gone to Dr Mumpzanmeazle but which the computer had donated to the Professor.

Mrs Flittersnoop didn't know about this either. She went to get some vegetables out of the back garden and when she came back to the kitchen she found the table was now a chair. Dr Mumpzanmeazle had brought the chair, which had been delivered to him instead of the table, and had taken away the table.

The chair *had* been ordered by Professor Branestawm. Not intentionally, of course. The Professor had been talking to Mr Chintsbitz, manager of the Pagwell

Furnishing Store, about being asked to take the chair at a meeting and the conversation had become rather muddled, so that the Professor had left Mr Chintsbitz with the idea that he wanted this particular chair.

'Now, let me see,' said Mrs Flittersnoop, looking all over the chair for knobs or levers which she couldn't find. 'I wonder how you turn this into a pair of steps or a table?'

She pulled its leg but nothing happened. She pushed it about and turned it upside down but still nothing happened.

'Well, I do think the Professor might have shown me how to work it,' she said. She sat down very gingerly on the chair, expecting it to collapse and turn into steps, but it didn't.

'You simply press this lever and the ladder automatically extends as required,' said the Professor.

He was explaining to Commander Hardaport (Retired) a special kind of mechanically extending ladder which the Professor thought might be useful to the Navy for getting to the top of tall masts instead of having to send sailors up on rope ladders. But of course they don't do it any more, except at naval training schools, because modern warships have hollow masts with lifts going up and down inside and television and gas fires and fitted carpets and coffee-making machines and all the other necessities of life.

'Still, you know what?' said the Commander, after he had explained all this to the Professor. 'I wouldn't mind having that ladder for getting at the apples at the top of my trees. All the best ones grow at the top out of reach, you know. Be very appropriate being able to go up the apples and pears to reach the apples and pears, ha! ha!'

'Well, er, yes,' said the Professor, who knew nothing whatever about rhyming slang and so didn't see the Commander's joke. But he felt it was rather a come-down for his marvellous automatic extending ladder, that was meant to help sustain the supremacy of the British Navy, to be used for picking a retired Commander's apples and pears. He began to wish he had shown it to Colonel Dedshott. At least the Colonel's head would have gone round and round at his explanations, but the Commander's head hadn't moved the least bit to port or starboard.

In fact Colonel Dedshott's head *was* going round and round at that very moment, because he was listening to Mrs Flittersnoop's explanations about the steps that turned into a table and became a chair.

'Never get the thing to work by ourselves, by Jove!' said the Colonel, after he and Mrs Flittersnoop had had several tries at converting the chair into steps. They had only succeeded in converting Mrs Flittersnoop's kitchen into a bit of a muddle, because the Colonel had trodden in the cat's breakfast and Mrs Flittersnoop had caught her elbow on the ironing board, which had tipped the kettle off the stove.

'Lawks a mussy me!' cried Mrs Flittersnoop. 'I don't

know why the Professor invents such awkward things, sir, I really don't.'

'Better wait till he gets back to explain,' grunted the Colonel. So they carried the chair to the Professor's inventory and left it there.

Professor Branestawm, round at Commander Hardaport's, was folding up his ladder.

'I fear you do not, ah, appreciate the advantages of my invention to the Navy, Commander,' he said. He shut the ladder up small and took it home.

'Perhaps Mrs Flittersnoop may find it useful for reaching high cupboards,' he said to himself, deciding that was better than reaching retired commanders' high apples and pears. He left the ladder in the kitchen and went into his inventory.

'Um, what's this?' he said, looking at the chair Colonel Dedshott had put there. 'I didn't order a chair. Really, these big stores are so, er, er . . . I shall tell them to take it back again.'

And so off he went to the Pagwell Furnishing Store, who hurriedly sent round for the chair without letting their computer know anything about it.

'Well, now, there don't appear to be no chair here,' said the Pagwell Furnishing man looking round the Professor's kitchen. 'But these here little steps looks to me just like what we brought here instead of taking to Mr Hokkibats's and what he's being going on a powerful lot about. Come on, Les, if we can't collect the chair as the Professor don't want and don't appear to have, we can take these here little steps along to Mr Hokki-bats.'

So he and Les whisked the Professor's closed-up mechanical ladder off to Mr Horace Hokkibats who was expecting some ordinary steps.

'Now I wonder what the Pagwell Furnishing Store called for,' thought Mrs Flittersnoop, who was upstairs making the beds and happened to glance out of the window and see the van leaving. She went downstairs and didn't find anything because, of course, the Pag-well Furnishing man and his friend, Les, had taken away the Professor's closed-up mechanical ladder which Mrs Flittersnoop didn't even know he had left there.

At the Pagwell Furnishing Store, Professor Brane-stawm was wandering about losing his way when he found himself in the Kitchen furniture department.

'Well, my goodness, this is most . . . tut, tut!' he mumbled. For he had caught sight of the little set of steps the store had delivered to his house by mistake and brought back again. And he thought it was his wonderful mechanical extending ladder folded into its smallest size.

'Dear! dear! This is most annoying!' he grunted. 'They've brought my invention here instead of collect-ing that chair they delivered which I didn't order.'

He picked up the steps and walked out, and nobody stopped him because the people at the Pagwell Furnish-ing Store were used to the Professor. They just put down

One set of kitchen steps on his account and thought no more about it.

'Oh, there you are sir,!' said Mrs Flittersnoop, when the Professor arrived home.

'Yes, where else should I be?' asked the Professor, thinking perhaps he should be somewhere else.

'Why, you've brought back the steps,' said Mrs Flittersnoop. 'The Colonel and I have been trying ever so hard to find out how they work, but now you're here, sir, you can show us.'

The Professor wondered how she could have known about his new invention but supposed he must have told her and forgotten.

'I'm longing to see how they turn into a table and then into a chair,' cried Mrs Flittersnoop, clapping her hands and moving everything out of the way.

'Table and chair?' said the Professor, pushing aside his pair of spectacles. 'This doesn't turn into a table and chair. It grows into a tall ladder for reaching up ships' masts. Let me show you.'

But, of course, he couldn't show her because what he had got was just an ordinary set of kitchen steps and not his invention at all. But just then Mrs Hokkibats arrived, in a terrible dither.

'Crisis, Professor!' she panted, waving her hands about. 'Come at once! My husband is stuck up on top of a great tall ladder and can't get down! You know all about these things, I've been told, so please come and rescue him. It was just a short little set of steps and the moment the poor man got on it, you know, *whoosh*, up it shot into a great long ladder! He can't get down and it's past time for his daily game of draughts, and he won't be able to practise for the staircase bowls tournament we're planning if something isn't done quickly!'

'Why, that must be my specially invented extending ladder your husband has!' said the Professor. 'I really don't understand how it came into his possession.'

Then Colonel Dedshott had a sudden attack of military intelligence.

'I see it, I see it, by Jove!' he cried, clapping his hand to his head and knocking his hat crooked. 'Did your husband order a little short set of steps from the Pagwell Furnishing Store?' he asked Mrs Hokkibats.

'Why, yes, he did,' she said. 'But they've sent this frightful contraption.'

'Then,' said Colonel Dedshott, putting his hat straight, 'these must be the steps your husband should have had.' He pointed to the kitchen steps the Professor had been trying unsuccessfully to extend. 'And your husband has Professor Branestawm's extending ladder.'

They all rushed round to the Hokkibats' house and the Professor soon got Horace down by collapsing the ladder and shooting Horace into a hole in the lawn.

'Jolly good shot, Professor! A hole in one!' he called cheerfully.

Then they left Mr Hokkibats to play with the ordinary little steps he had ordered, and took the Professor's marvellous extending ladder back for Mrs Flittersnoop to use to reach the top cupboards.

'Thank you very much, I'm sure, sir,' she said. She felt a bit disappointed that the ladder wouldn't turn into a table for writing out shopping lists or a chair for sitting on to think out shopping lists. But at least she was able to reach the top cupboards, where she found rows and rows of things she hadn't seen for a long time, most of which the Professor had put up there when he was trying to be helpful, which it is always a mistake for gentlemen to try to be in the kitchen.

11

Strictly for the Birds

'Shoo!' roared Farmer Plownough. 'Scram! Vamoose! Get away with ye!'

He waved his arms frantically at the crowd of birds that were having a lovely time eating his seeds.

'Be off with ye now, and don't be a-coming back!' he shouted, waving his arms again until he looked like a bird himself.

The birds flew away, but no sooner had he begun to walk towards the farmhouse than back they all came with a lot of friends and relations as well.

'Arrh, this do be too bad,' grunted the Farmer, and he went in to tea to worry about it.

'Why don't we have a scarecrow?' asked Mrs Plownough.

'Scarecrow!' cried the Farmer. 'Why, I've got a fine scarecrow over in the five acre field. The birds love it, they do. They perch on it to eat the seed they've taken. They shelter from the rain in it. They do build their nests in it, an all. A lot of good that do be as a scarecrow!'

'Perhaps they don't know it's a scarecrow,' said Mrs Plownough. 'Perhaps they don't know they should be a-scared of it?'

'What do ee suggest then?' said the Farmer, starting on his fifth piece of cake because farming is hungry work. 'Put a notice on it saying, *Warning, scarecrow. Birds strictly prohibited?*'

Just then there was a knock at the door.

'If that be those darned birds calling for more seed, tell em they can't have it!' growled the Farmer.

But it wasn't the birds. It was Professor Branestawm, with all his five pairs of spectacles and his hat on the wrong way round.

'Ah, good afternoon,' said the Professor. 'Mrs Flittersnoop was wondering whether you could let us have some wandering eggs.'

'Wandering eggs?' said the Farmer. 'What do they be?'

'Sit down and have a cup of tea, now, do,' said Mrs Plownough, cutting a fresh cake for the Professor as the Farmer had eaten all the first one.

'Er, yes,' said the Professor. 'They taste better than those battery-operated ones, I believe.'

'Ha, you means free range eggs,' said the Farmer. 'Well, I reckon as we can let you have some, that is, if the missus can find out where they darned birds has laid em, they being a bit too free-ranging at times, like.'

'Perhaps the Professor could help us about the birds?' said Mrs Plownough.

'Ah, now, yes, if I might make so bold as to ask for your help,' said the Farmer. 'You being a clever gentleman as invents things, so to speak.'

And as he told the Professor about the birds and the

scarecrow that couldn't scare sparrows, let alone crows, and how he didn't know what to do at all.

'Ah,' said the Professor, putting a piece of cake on his nose in mistake for spectacles. 'Why, yes, I think I understand the problem. Birds are scared of anything unusual, but if the unusual happens regularly, then it becomes usual and they are no longer scared of it. That is why,' he went on, ticking off points on his fingers and upsetting his tea, 'when you waved your arms and shouted you became unusual, and the birds were frightened and flew away. But when you kept on shouting and waving your arms, this eventually became a usual thing and so the birds were no longer scared of it.'

'Ah, now,' said Farmer Plownough. 'Then that do be why the old scarecrow over in the five acre field don't scare the birds. They be used to him, like.'

'Of course,' said the Professor. 'Now what we have to do is to invent a scarecrow that will always be unusual, no matter what it does. A scarecrow that will keep doing unusual things at all sorts of odd times. The birds,' the Professor leant forward and his spectacles fell off into the jam, 'must not be allowed to guess what the scarecrow will do next or when it will do it. We must have an unpredictable scarecrow.'

He sat back and Farmer Plownough said, 'Ah, that do be fine with me, Professor. You invent me one of the unpredictable scarecrows.'

And so Professor Branestawm went home to invent an unpredictable scarecrow.

*

'Now, let me think,' said the Professor, back in his inventory. And, as there was nobody there to stop him, he thought.

'What things can a scarecrow do that are unusual, and how can it do them at unusual times so that the birds will not be expecting it?'

Just then there was a loud bang outside. It wasn't one of the Professor's inventions. It was a motor car backfiring. But it banged an idea into the Professor's head.

'Ha!' he exclaimed. 'A scarecrow that fires a gun! Yes, and at different intervals of time. And in case the birds become immunized against gunfire, I shall make my scarecrow sing songs, fierce ones. It can also wave flags, let off fireworks, operate flashing lights. Um, yes. This is going to be a scarecrow to shake the farming world.'

He set to work. He got Mrs Flittersnoop to give him an old coat of hers and a discarded hat. He used a photograph of Colonel Dedshott at his fiercest for the face. He built into the scarecrow a patent machine gun firing blanks, a mini flame-thrower, several illuminated signs that Ginnibag & Knitwoddle had finished with, a stereo radio, a second-hand trombone, a tape recorder, an egg whisk and fourteen yards of black hat elastic.

When at last he had the scarecrow finished it sounded like a cross between a pop festival and the Catapult Cavaliers attacking the Salvation Army (which of course they never did). It had fourteen arms, and each arm

did something different and all of them did something outrageous.

'Well, now, that do be summat like a scarecrow, that do be!' exclaimed Farmer Plownough, when the Professor took his invention over to the farm.

'Jolly clever, my word!' said Colonel Dedshott, who had come along in case the scarecrow needed to be given any orders.

They set it up in the middle of a field.

'I will now switch it on,' said the Professor. He pressed a switch.

Bang! Bang! Bang! Bang! the scarecrow opened fire immediately.

They ran across the field and hid behind some bushes. The scarecrow did nothing more, and presently the field was full of birds.

'It don't work,' Farmer Plownough began to say, when the scarecrow suddenly shot out a yard of flame, played *The British Grenadiers* backwards, let off three rockets and a catherine wheel, fired another salvo and finished up with a severe talk on stomach ache.

The birds instantly rose in a shower and vanished.

'My word, that do be something!' chuckled the Farmer, and Colonel Dedshott said, 'Hrrrm!' just to show that the Professor's inventions were nothing new to him, which of course they weren't.

Then the birds came back. But the scarecrow saw them and treated them to a Spagletonian Rain Dance, which fortunately produced no rain as the Professor hadn't brought an umbrella.

The birds flew off again and, just as they were thinking it might be safe to come down once more, the Professor's scarecrow gave a series of military commands which caused Colonel Dedshott to jump to attention without thinking.

'Pah!' he snorted, and scared away two innocent robins who had no desire at all to eat the Farmer's seed's but were looking for worms under a nearby bush.

'Well, I think we have solved the problem of your birds,' said the Professor, and he went home with Colonel Dedshott, leaving Farmer Plownough delighted that his crops were safe.

Professor Branestawm was in the middle of getting ready to think about an invention when galloping hoofs sounded outside.

'Ha, Dedshott!' cried the Professor. 'Come in!'

But it wasn't Colonel Dedshott. It was Farmer Plownough on his best and biggest horse and in a real panic.

'Things do be terrible down at the farm!' he panted.

'Dear me!' said the Professor. 'I, er, trust my, um, ah, scarecrow has not, er, er . . .'

'Ho, no, that scarecrow be a-working all right,' said the Farmer, shaking his head. 'I don't have no more trouble with the birds. It's the people I'm worried at now.'

'I had better go over to the farm and see what the situation really is,' said the Professor. He went round to collect Colonel Dedshott and they all returned to the farm.

'By Jove, what!' exclaimed the Colonel, when they arrived. 'What's this, queuing up for free-ranging eggs or something?'

There wasn't a bird in sight on Farmer Plownough's land, but the place was packed with people.

'They've come to see the scarecrow,' cried Farmer Plownough, pushing his way through the crowd.

'Most gratifying, most gratifying,' said the Professor. 'I must say I am very glad to see that one of my inventions is appreciated by the public. And you see,' he began ticking off the points on his fingers, 'now even if the scarecrow should become usual to the birds, the people who come to see it are not usual, so the birds will be afraid of them. And as the people keep moving and new ones keep coming the whole situation will continue to be unusual to the birds. I do not think you will have anything more to worry about.'

But, if the Professor thought Farmer Plownough's life was going to be one long unworrying joy, he had to think again, though, as a Professor, thinking again was something he was quite good at.

'The people coming to see the scarecrow do be doing more damage to my land than the birds they scare away,' complained the Farmer. 'So now what's to do? If I have the scarecrow they folk'll be all trampling my crops for to look at ee, and if I don't have the scarecrow they birds'll be back eating all the seeds.'

'You must charge admission,' said the Professor, who suddenly remembered that Pagwell Council had made some useful money charging to see his mechanical monster in Pagwell Lake.

'Ah, now,' said the Farmer. 'Yes, that do be an idea. How much do ee think, Professor? Twenty pence for adults and children half price?'

'Well,' said the Professor. 'You'll have to be careful about children half price, because, if one child comes in for half price, that means two children can come in for no price at all, and if more than two children come in you will owe them something. And,' he went on, getting excited, 'if a lot of children come to see the scarecrow you might find yourself paying out a great deal of money. It might be cheaper to let the birds in again.'

But Farmer Plownough was off, and soon had notices saying, *See the wonderful mechanical scarecrow! Only one of its kind! Admission 20p.*

That did it. The people stopped coming, possibly because they thought they could see funnier scarecrows in the streets of Pagwell without paying. And by then it was harvest time anyway and Farmer Plownough gathered in the crops, so there was nothing for the birds to take, or the people to trample.

'Well, thank goodness for that,' said Mrs Plownough.

'Oh, ah,' said the Farmer. 'But what's going to happen in a few years' time when the birds get used to the Professor's scarecrow?' Farmers have to have something to worry about.

But Professor Branestawm was already dealing with that problem. He was working on astonishing inventions for roofing in the farm with transparent material that would let the sunshine in but keep the birds out, and with holes in it to let the rain through but not the birds.

And during the winter months Farmer Plownough hired out the wonderful automatic scarecrow to the Great Pagwell Amusement Arcade where they set it up in a special room and charged ten pence to see it. And as people didn't mind spending ten pence to see it when they didn't get their feet muddy it was a great success.

12

Professor Branestawm's Great Revolution

REVOLUTION was in the air in Great Pagwell. Good
gracious! Did that mean revolting Councillors were
staging a sit-in in the Town Hall? Was Colonel Dedshott marshalling the Catapult Cavaliers to repulse
insurgent plumbers? Were the Pagwell housewives going to march?

No, it wasn't that kind of revolution at all. It was
simply that the Mayor and Professor Branestawm were
discussing the question of whether Great Pagwell ought
to have a revolving restaurant on top of a tower. And
they were discussing this revolutionary question very
properly over dinner in the non-revolving restaurant
of Great Pagwell Hotel.

'Great Pagwell already has a number of very notable
features,' said the Mayor, accepting from Monsieur
Bonmonjay, the hotel manager, a choice steak, char-
coal-grilled to perfection. 'It has a new Town Hall
unlike any other town hall,' he went on.

'That was due to arguments among architects,' said
Professor Branestawm.

'And,' went on the Mayor, 'it has a lake with an
automatic monster, on view daily. And we have the
famous and unique underground yacht basin, another

of your inventions, my dear Professor. But the point is,' he wagged his fork and scattered a blob of wine sauce on the Professor's nose, 'the point is, Great Pagwell does not have a revolving restaurant.'

'Of course not,' said the Professor, blinking his eyes behind his five pairs of spectacles as waiters with trolleys shot past.

'I think we should have one,' said the Mayor.

'Thank you,' said the Professor, as a trolley load of ice-creams drew up beside them.

'I mean, we should have a revolving restaurant on a tower,' said the Mayor. 'And you, my dear Professor, are just the man to invent one for us.'

'I am, um, well,' said the Professor. 'It's been done before, you know. A lot of towns have revolving restaurants, I believe.'

'Of course they have,' said the Mayor, lighting his cigar. 'Every self-respecting town has a revolving restaurant on a tower. That's why I say Great Pagwell should have one.'

'But,' protested the Professor, 'I don't invent things that have been done before. I am unique.' He waved his spoon and gave the people at the next table a free cherry.

'Well, you could invent an entirely different kind of revolving restaurant, I am sure, Professor,' said the Mayor.

The argument went on and on, with the Mayor offering one reason after another why the Professor should place Great Pagwell in the forefront of modern civilized towns by giving it a revolving restaurant. And he talked so much and made so many complicated points, that at last it was settled, and Professor Branestawm went home via East Pagwell, Pagwell Heights and Pagwell-by-the-Water because he was thinking so much about revolving restaurants he took the wrong exit at seven roundabouts.

'What's this?' cried Commander Hardaport (Retired), opening his post at breakfast several weeks later. '*Opening of Great Pagwell's New Revolving Restaurant on Pagwell Point Lighthouse*?' His nautical mind revolved at several revs per minute. Surely this would constitute a danger to shipping? Revolving restaurants on top of lighthouses? The sailors would be confused. Ships would run aground. The lifeboat would be called out, and Great Pagwell didn't have a lifeboat.

'Stop engines!' roared the Commander, suddenly seeing light. 'Of course, Pagwell Point Lighthouse is not in commission any more.'

It was true. The lighthouse had been built centuries ago and at that time the land where Great Pagwell stands was by the sea-side. Since then the sea had slowly sunk back and left the lighthouse miles and miles inland, which made it look a bit silly. It had been used in turn as a place for firemen to practice jumping off into sheets, a skywalk for people to admire the view until Pagwell Gasworks made the view rather unadmirable, and a vertical Bingo Hall.

Commander Hardaport made up his mind to go to

the grand opening. He felt a restaurant on top of a lighthouse was very fitting place for a naval Commander to take on provisions.

The Vicar also decided to go, accompanied by his twin daughters, Daisie and Maisie, and began wondering if a revolving restaurant attracted a lot of customers whether a revolving church might attract bigger congregations.

Dr Mumpzanmeazle reckoned that he was always doing his rounds anyway, he might as well go round while having dinner too.

Colonel Dedshott was of course used to meals on the move but thought a seat in a revolving restaurant might be more comfortable, if less military, than one on a moving horse.

'You must accompany me to the scene of my latest triumph, er, Mrs Flittersnoop,' said the Professor.

'Thank you, sir, I should like to, I'm sure,' said Mrs Flittersnoop. She had experienced so many revolutions in meal-times for the Professor that she felt she would be quite at home in a revolving restaurant.

So the opening night of the Great Pagwell Revolving Restaurant and Top-of-the-Town Nightspot was well attended. Most of the important people in Pagwell were there, and a great many who thought they were important, as well as some who really were, like the chefs who cooked the dinner and the waiters who served it.

The Mayor stood up and was just going to say, 'I

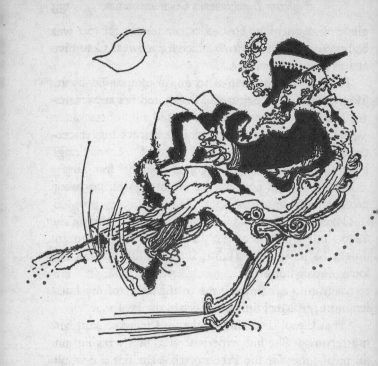

have pleasure in declaring this revolving restaurant open,' when the restaurant started revolving, with a slight jerk that sat him down again.

'It's just like having dinner on a train,' said Mrs Flittersnoop, watching the lights of Lower Pagwell drift slowly past.

'Well, it's a change to have the restaurant high as well as the prices,' said Dr Mumpzanmeazle, doing complicated surgical operations on a large flat steak.

Commander Hardaport, champing nautically on a

piece of rather truculent pork crackling, felt he was back on the bridge of a battleship and wanted to give orders what course to set.

'Bravo, Branestawm!' declared Colonel Dedshott, feeling quite at home as the flames from a *crêpe suzette* went off like an enthusiastic cannon.

Just then a young waiter dropped a plateful of extremely French food into the works, and peculiar things began to happen.

The restaurant continued to revolve with becoming dignity, but the tables began to revolve too, each on its own axis. Unfortunately the chairs stayed where they were so that everybody began to get someone else's dinner. The Vicar, who always had fish on Friday, found himself opposite a rare steak. Vegetarians were returned to other people's muttons, and strict teetotallers were given large glasses of wine.

'Avast there!' roared Commander Hardaport, glaring down at a round trifle with almonds sticking out all over it that reminded him too much of a floating mine. He dashed across to investigate the machinery, and bumped into Professor Branestawm, who was fiddling with levers. The collision put him off course and he pulled two wrong levers. Immediately the restaurant began to speed up. The tables spun round, sending delicious food of all kinds hurtling across the floor. The whole restaurant began to whirl round like a mad roundabout.

'Down revs!' roared the Commander, pulling more wrong levers than the Professor.

Colonel Dedshott fought his way through a flank attack of meringues to come to the rescue.

The restaurant put on a few more knots and took off from the top of the lighthouse.

'Flying saucer, by gad!' roared Colonel Dedshott, who didn't agree with unidentified flying objects, especially when he was in one of them.

Zoom! The revolving restaurant, now a flying and revolving restaurant, shot into the air and made for the coast.

'Man the lifeboats!' roared Commander Hardaport, but there weren't any.

'Oh, my goodness me!' wailed Mrs Flittersnoop, trying to hide under a revolving table.

'We're heading for the sea!' roared Commander Hardaport. 'Change course, Branestawm, or we'll be down in the shipping lanes.'

'Ah, um, er, er, yes,' spluttered the Professor, groping for levers under the floor, and being hampered on every side by spaghetti and bouncing Brussels sprouts.

At last he managed to pull a lever, but it was the wrong one. The revolving mechanism stopped and the restaurant began falling straight down.

'Out parachutes!' roared Commander Hardaport.

Mrs Flittersnoop, still under the table, tried to put up her umbrella.

The Vicar composed five entirely new prayers and said all of them at once.

Down rushed the restaurant. The food shot up and stuck to the ceiling.

The Professor pulled three levers and five steaks. The motors started up again. The restaurant began to spin round just as it hit the sea.

'Abandon ship!' shouted Commander Hardaport.

But, good gracious, the now rapidly revolving restaurant skidded across the top of the waves like a hovercraft, slid up the beach and came to rest right on the promenade of a seaside resort.

'Well, thank goodness we're down safely,' said the Professor, getting out and helping Mrs Flittersnoop to escape from the table.

'Now then, what's all this?' said a voice, and a large policeman appeared.

'It's Professor Branestawm's revolving restaurant,' said the Vicar. 'We have, I'm afraid, come down here by mistake.'

'Well, you can't leave it here,' said the policeman, taking out a notebook.

'I fear it will be impossible to, um, ah, take off again,' said the Professor, emerging from the machinery. 'I shall have to make arrangements for it to be collected later.'

'I shall have to book you for illegal parking, then,' said the policeman, making notes.

'As far as I know there is no law saying one must not park a revolving restaurant on a seaside promenade,' said the Professor.

The policeman scratched his head. 'Now you mention it, I don't think there is,' he said. 'But I can book you for obstruction.'

'We have a licence to sell alcoholic liquor,' said the Professor, hoping that made a difference. 'And a revolving restaurant is not a vehicle within the meaning of the act.'

The policeman refreshed himself with another lick at his pencil and was about to utter further legal remarks when two gentlemen arrived.

'We represent the Splashmidoo-on-Sea Rural Council,' they said, speaking together and raising their hats together. 'Is this Professor Branestawm?'

'Er, yes,' said the Professor. 'I'm afraid my new revolving restaurant has inadvertently landed on your promenade. I, um, er, that is to say . . .'

'Please don't worry, Professor,' said the superior gentlemen. 'Splashmidoo-on-Sea has long needed a sun lounge and restaurant on the promenade and for many years we have been trying to raise sufficient funds. If you care to present this edifice to the town, we shall be more than happy to say no more about it.'

So the Professor's marvellous and almost unbelievable revolving restaurant became Splashmidoo-on-Sea's delightful popular seaside sun restaurant.

And, thank goodness, apart from the spot of bother the Professor and his friends had in getting home to Great Pagwell from Splashmidoo-on-Sea in the middle of the night, all was well that ended so unexpectedly.